The Poison Belt

Arthur Conan Doyle

ET REMOTISSIMA PROPE

Modern Voices

Modern Voices
Published by Hesperus Press Limited
4 Rickett Street, London sw6 1RU
www.hesperuspress.com

First published in 1913
First published by Hesperus Press Limited, 2008

Whilst the text of *The Poison Belt* has been reproduced as per the
original edition, the opinions expressed within it by no means reflect
those of the publisher.

Foreword © Matthew Sweet, 2008

Designed and typeset by Fraser Muggeridge studio
Printed in Jordan by the Jordan National Press

ISBN: 978-1-84391-182-1

Contents

Foreword

On the day that the guns fell silent in the trenches and the church bells rang all over England, Sir Arthur Conan Doyle received the most painful blow of his life. His eldest son, a captain in the First Hampshire Regiment, had breathed his last. The news was not unexpected: Kingsley had been wounded at the Somme and his damaged lungs had since buckled under attacks of pneumonia and Spanish flu. Nor was there much unusual in his father's response to the bereavement. In common with many parents who lost their children in the Great War, Doyle assuaged his grief in a dark room with a psychic medium at his side. He hoped for a last conversation with his lost son. He hoped for evidence that death was a more equivocal state than his medical studies had insisted. And as far as he was concerned, his hopes were fulfilled. 'My boy tried to console me at his death,' he reported. 'He referred to other friends who had passed over and said: "When I was alive I did not believe in spiritualism. Now I believe in it. I was a chuckle-headed ass not to believe it."'

Some pinned the tail on a different donkey. *Truth* magazine considered that Mrs B had 'consciously humbugged Sir Arthur Conan Doyle and twenty-four of the twenty-six people he has sent to her.' It was probably true. Doyle's interest in communicating with the dead – the great obsession of his last years – did not earn him much respect in his lifetime and has remained a source of embarrassment to his posthumous champions. Along with his belief in fairies, ectoplasm and telepathy, it offends those who admire him so much for having created the hyper-rational detective Sherlock Holmes. 'I have an occasional power of premonition,' Doyle wrote, 'psychic rather than intellectual, which exercises itself beyond my own control, and when it really comes is never mistaken.' One can imagine Holmes dismissing such claims with a flick of the wrist and a contemptuous *pshaw*.

But perhaps the book you have in your hands might have made him think again.

The Poison Belt was published a year before the Great War reduced a vast tract of Europe to a wasteland of mud and corpses. The novella depicts a sunlit, complacent world drifting heedlessly towards oblivion, deaf to the doomsday prophecies of its hero. It describes a global catastrophe, panic on the streets, populations scythed down by the million. It follows a small band of survivors through the silent streets of London, where the pavements are littered with bodies and the roads occluded by motionless cars and wagons. It imagines the details of an English Armageddon, in which Home Counties golfers collapse on the fairway; London newsvendors crumple over their stacks of papers; lifeless schoolchildren strew the playground.

To me, as an early twenty-first century reader, these images suggest that the Angel of Death has arrived a year or so too early, to save a generation of British men the fuss and bother of polishing their brass buttons, waving their handkerchiefs from train windows and marching down country lanes all the way to the fields of Flanders. But they also conjure another image in my mind: a page from *Our Dumb Century* (1999), a publication by the creators of the satirical magazine, *The Onion*, which offered mock coverage of the Titanic disaster of 1912. The headline ran: 'World's Largest Metaphor Hits Ice-Berg'.

The prophet of doom in *The Poison Belt* is Professor George Edward Challenger – the bullish, domineering, self-regarding scientific genius whom, a year previously, Doyle had dispatched on a dinosaur hunt through the Brazilian jungle. In *The Lost World* (1912), Challenger and his comrades ascend a plateau high above the rainforest, upon which evolution has taken a resolutely retro turn: iguanadon still rule supreme; stegosaurus spikes and plates remain fashionable; pterodactyls lose no sleep over being outevolved by birds. *The Poison Belt* creates another isolated bubble of existence; another elevated Galapagos on which the inhabitants elude the influence of the broader world. This time, however, the plateau is a comfortable brick villa on the edge of the Sussex Downs – and Challenger and his associates are playing the part of the pterodactyls.

Ether is the substance that casts them in these roles – an invisible fluid that, for much of the nineteenth century, was imagined to occupy the space between physical bodies: stars, planets, trees, mountains, people. Occam's razor had been slashing away at the concept of ether since 1887, when an experiment devised by two scientists called Michelson and Morley to test its qualities produced results suggesting that it did not exist at all. In 1907, Albert Michelson was awarded the Nobel Prize for having evacuated ether from theoretical space.

That fact did not concern Conan Doyle. In *The Poison Belt*, a bank of toxic ether is billowing through the void and the earth is directly in its path. The ether is tasteless, odourless, deadly – and only Professor Challenger has detected its presence. As the planet is submerged in this poisonous flood, populations begin to expire in the pecking order ascribed to them by early twentieth-century eugenic anthropology. Sumatrans, Africans and Aboriginal Australians wobble and fall first; sturdy northern European white folks are the last men standing. ('The Slavonic population of Austria is down,' reports a news cable, 'while the Teutonic has hardly been affected.') The Professor's party barricades itself inside Mrs Challenger's boudoir and hopes that a crate of hissing oxygen cylinders will keep the deadly agent at bay. 'Even our own little hill,' reasons the Professor, 'may presently prove to be a temporary island in a sea of disaster.' The servants are not invited. The possibility of saving them is never discussed. As the poison belt tightens around the earth, Challenger's chauffeur, Austin, is permitted to fall senseless to the gravel in the act of washing the car.

Sir Arthur Conan Doyle was not the first author to kill everybody in the world. Mary Shelley mothered an early literary genocide in 1828 when she sent the protagonist of *The Last Man* exploring a plague-ravaged earth. But the catastrophe that exerts the most powerful influence upon *The Poison Belt* is one staged in a strange novel by Matthew Phipps Shiel, a prolific and eccentric writer who specialised in the outré and the grotesque. In *The Purple Cloud* (1901), an Arctic explorer called Adam Jeffson becomes the first human to gaze upon the North Pole – which, with delightful literalism, is revealed to be a giant pillar of ice protruding from the middle of a freezing lake. The pillar bears an inscription: a forbidden name written, presumably, by the hand of God. Adam's discovery of this structure triggers a bizarre cosmic booby-trap: as he gazes upon the Pole, a Krakatoa of lurid poison gas erupts from a volcano in the Pacific and gushes across the face of the globe, delousing the planet of its entire human and animal populations. Human curiosity is punished. World's Largest Metaphor Hits Ice-Berg.

The events of *The Poison Belt* take place in a colder universe – one in which divine forces have not lavished sufficient attention upon humanity to formulate as bizarre and elaborate a punishment as a toxic Purple Cloud. As doomsday approaches, Challenger asks his comrades to imagine the earth as a bunch of grapes infected with bacteria. 'The Great Gardener has sterilised the human mould which had grown over the surface of His fruit.' In this hypothesis, the extermination of human life is not the whoop-de-do finale of a sadistic celestial plan. It is the casual Sunday afternoon activity of a creator who cares little for us – or a random event in an utterly chaotic universe in which humanity enjoys no particular significance.

This kind of philosophical despair is natural to this period, and it had been a long time coming: Copernicus had banished humanity to the frowsty edges of the solar system; Darwin had recast the human race as a collection of well-dressed apes; Marx had put individuals at the mercy of chill historical forces; Nietzsche had nailed down the lid on God's coffin; new approaches to physics were reshaping old ideas about the nature of time and space. Western culture left the nineteenth century with a new cognisance of its own marginality. In *The Poison Belt*, Challenger describes the dream from which his species has just awoken: 'It is as if the scum on the surface of the ocean imagined that it was created in order to produce and sustain it, or a mouse in a cathedral thought that the building was its own proper ordained residence.' These were the perfect conditions for the propagation of new cosmologies, new mysticisms, new doctrines about life, death and the soul. Spiritualism was ready to flower. All that was required was millions of bereaved people. The Somme obliged.

However much the cataclysm that followed its publication might now seem to haunt Doyle's story, *The Poison Belt* was not written to warn its readers of the inevitability of a bloody military smash-up on the Continent. In the summer of 1913, a few months after his story had appeared in the *Strand* magazine, Doyle published an article in the *Fortnightly Review*, in which he argued that war between Britain and Germany was eminently avoidable. 'I have never seriously believed in the German menace,' he declared. 'Frequently I have found myself alone in a company of educated Englishmen in my opinion that it was non-existent – or at least greatly exaggerated.' Democracy, he reasoned, would save Europe from destruction, as the enfranchised proletariat would not be persuaded to fix their bayonets and charge, shouting, towards each other. And if some insane element within the Berlin government did succeed in mobilising the nation, then Britain could ensure effective resistance by commissioning one grand engineering project: a Channel tunnel, through which the country might keep itself supplied with food from the Mediterranean. It was an article upon which Doyle would look back with mixed feelings. 'It lies before me now,' he wrote in his autobiography, *Memories and Adventures* (1924), 'and it is interesting to see how, as I projected my mind and my imagination over the possibilities of the future, I read much aright and some little wrong.'

That matters little. The real value of *The Poison Belt* is not in the efficacy of its crystal-gazing, but in its exploration of the mechanics of early twentieth-century despair. Does it matter if we live or die? Does it matter if our neighbours live or die? What difference would it make to the universe if our entire species were all snuffed out in the course of an afternoon? The book's answers are equivocal. Doyle, however, seems certain about one thing: that the most dread state of hopelessness need not be absolute – even a state as seemingly immutable as death.

Some readers picked up on this notion with enthusiasm. In May 1920, the art critic M.H. Spielmann wrote a letter to *The Times* in which he suggested that western culture was sunk in a strange, unhealthy period. 'We have,' he argued, 'been passing through Sir Arthur Conan Doyle's brilliantly imagined "Poison Belt" – the poison belt of dementia – of which the maddest and crowning symptom has been the Great War itself. We must recognise that when the world and its inhabitants regain their equilibrium, and not before, will men – artists and others – awaken to the absurdities and horrors under which we are groaning.'

When war came, Arthur Conan Doyle threw away hopes for Anglo-German friendship and applied himself with ferocity to the problem of ensuring Allied victory. He used his own money to fund a branch of the Civilian Reserve, a militia in the manner of the Home Guard. He lobbied the War Office with tireless energy and some success, arguing that sailors should be equipped with inflatable lifejackets and front-line soldiers with body armour. He wrote a propaganda pamphlet, *To Arms* (1914), which fulminated against the 'swaggering Junkerdom of Prussia'. He visited the Western Front as a war correspondent, sharing tea with servicemen before they went over the top. And the more the death toll clicked upwards, the more interested he became in the fate of those lost souls, and whether it might still be possible to contact them. He was in Nottingham giving a lecture on the power of spiritualism when he received a telegram from his daughter informing him that Kingsley Conan Doyle was dying. He shed a few discreet tears, then went out to address his audience. A report of Kingsley's final moments reached his father on Armistice Day.

Today we commemorate that original Armistice Day with a ritual that may come to mind as you read the last pages of *The Poison Belt*. On an appointed hour on the second Sunday morning each November, tracts of England fall suddenly silent. From Admiralty Arch to the Houses of Parliament, London holds its breath. Whitehall becomes a mass of stilled human bodies. Nothing stirs, except memories of the war dead – Kingsley Conan Doyle among them, perhaps. Then, a cannon sounds. The air exhales. Those stilled bodies return to life. And the earth spins on through an indifferent universe.

– *Matthew Sweet, 2008*

The Poison Belt

Being an account of another adventure of
Prof. George E. Challenger, Lord John Roxton,
Prof. Summerlee, and Mr. E.D. Malone,
the discoverers of 'The Lost World'

The Blurring of the Lines

It is imperative that now at once, while these stupendous events are still clear in my mind, I should set them down with that exactness of detail which time may blur. But even as I do so, I am overwhelmed by the wonder of the fact that it should be our little group of the 'Lost World' – Professor Challenger, Professor Summerlee, Lord John Roxton, and myself – who have passed through this amazing experience.

When, some years ago, I chronicled in the *Daily Gazette* our epoch-making journey in South America, I little thought that it should ever fall to my lot to tell an even stranger personal experience, one which is unique in all human annals, and must stand out in the records of history as a great peak among the humble foothills which surround it. The event itself will always be marvellous, but the circumstances that we four were together at the time of this extraordinary episode came about in a most natural and, indeed, inevitable fashion. I will explain the events which led up to it as shortly and as clearly as I can, though I am well aware that the fuller the detail upon such a subject the more welcome it will be to the reader, for the public curiosity has been and still is insatiable.

It was upon Friday, the twenty-seventh of August – a date forever memorable in the history of the world – that I went down to the office of my paper and asked for three days' leave of absence from Mr McArdle, who still presided over our news department. The good old Scotchman shook his head, scratched his dwindling fringe of ruddy fluff, and finally put his reluctance into words.

'I was thinking, Mr Malone, that we could employ you to advantage these days. I was thinking there was a story that you are the only man that could handle as it should be handled.'

'I am sorry for that,' said I, trying to hide my disappointment. 'Of course if I am needed, there is an end of the matter. But the engagement was important and intimate. If I could be spared –'

'Well, I don't see that you can.'

It was bitter, but I had to put the best face I could upon it. After all, it was my own fault, for I should have known by this time that a journalist has no right to make plans of his own.

'Then I'll think no more of it,' said I with as much cheerfulness as I could assume at so short a notice. 'What was it that you wanted me to do?'

'Well, it was just to interview that deevil of a man down at Rotherfield.'

'You don't mean Professor Challenger?' I cried.

'Aye, it's just him that I do mean. He ran young Alec Simpson, of the *Courier*, a mile down the high road last week by the collar of his coat and the slack of his breeches. You'll have read of it, likely, in the police report. Our boys would as soon interview a loose alligator in the zoo. But you could do it, I'm thinking – an old friend like you.'

'Why,' said I, greatly relieved, 'this makes it all easy. It so happens that it was to visit Professor Challenger at Rotherfield that I was asking for leave of absence. The fact is, that it is the anniversary of our main adventure on the plateau three years ago, and he has asked our whole party down to his house to see him and celebrate the occasion.'

'Capital!' cried McArdle, rubbing his hands and beaming through his glasses. 'Then you will be able to get his opeenions out of him. In any other man I would say it was all moonshine, but the fellow has made good once, and who knows but he may again!'

'Get what out of him?' I asked. 'What has he been doing?'

'Haven't you seen his letter on "Scientific Possibeelities" in today's *Times*?'

'No.'

McArdle dived down and picked a copy from the floor.

'Read it aloud,' said he, indicating a column with his finger. 'I'd be glad to hear it again, for I am not sure now that I have the man's meaning clear in my head.'

This was the letter which I read to the news editor of the *Gazette*:–

'SCIENTIFIC POSSIBILITIES'

Sir, I have read with amusement, not wholly unmixed with some less complimentary emotion, the complacent and wholly fatuous letter of James Wilson MacPhail which has lately appeared in your columns upon the subject of the blurring of Fraunhofer's lines in the spectra both of the planets and of the fixed stars. He dismisses the matter as of no significance. To a wider intelligence it may well seem of very great possible importance – so great as to involve the ultimate welfare of every man, woman, and child upon this planet. I can hardly hope, by the use of scientific language, to convey any sense of my meaning to those ineffectual people who gather their ideas from the columns of a daily newspaper. I will endeavour, therefore, to condescend to their limitation and to indicate the situation by the use of a homely analogy which will be within the limits of the intelligence of your readers.

'Man, he's a wonder – a living wonder!' said McArdle, shaking his head reflectively. 'He'd put up the feathers of a sucking-dove and set up a riot in a Quakers' meeting. No wonder he has made London too hot for him. It's a peety, Mr Malone, for it's a grand brain! Well, let's have the analogy.'

We will suppose, I read, *that a small bundle of connected corks was launched in a sluggish current upon a voyage across the Atlantic. The corks drift slowly on from day to day with the same conditions all round them. If the corks were sentient we could imagine that they would consider these conditions to be permanent and assured. But we, with our superior knowledge, know that many things might happen to surprise the corks. They might possibly float up against a ship, or a sleeping whale, or become entangled in seaweed. In any case, their voyage would probably end by their being thrown up on the rocky coast of Labrador. But what could they know of all this while they drifted so gently day by day in what they thought was a limitless and homogeneous ocean?*

Your readers will possibly comprehend that the Atlantic, in this parable, stands for the mighty ocean of ether through which we drift, and that the bunch of corks represents the little and obscure planetary system to which we belong. A third-rate sun, with its rag-tag and bobtail of insignificant satellites, we float under the same daily conditions towards some unknown end, some squalid catastrophe which will overwhelm us at the ultimate confines of space, where we are swept over an etheric Niagara or dashed upon some unthinkable Labrador. I see no room here for the shallow and ignorant optimism of your correspondent, Mr James Wilson MacPhail, but many reasons why we should watch with a very close and interested attention every indication of change in those cosmic surroundings upon which our own ultimate fate may depend.

'Man, he'd have made a grand meenister,' said McArdle. 'It just booms like an organ. Let's get doun to what it is that's troubling him.'

The general blurring and shifting of Fraunhofer's lines of the spectrum point, in my opinion, to a widespread cosmic change of a subtle and singular character. Light from a planet is the reflected light of the sun. Light from a star is a self-produced light. But the spectra both from planets and stars have, in this instance, all undergone the same change. Is it, then, a change in those planets and stars? To me such an idea is inconceivable. What common change could simultaneously come upon them all? Is it a change in our own atmosphere? It is possible, but in the highest degree improbable, since we see no signs of it around us, and chemical analysis has failed to reveal it. What, then, is the third possibility? That it may be a change in the conducting medium, in that infinitely fine ether which extends from star to star and pervades the whole universe. Deep in that ocean we are floating upon a slow current. Might that current not drift us into belts of ether which are novel and have properties of which we have never conceived? There is a change somewhere. This cosmic disturbance of the spectrum proves it. It may be a good change. It may be an evil one. It may be a neutral one. We do not know. Shallow observers may treat the matter as one which can be disregarded, but one who like myself is possessed of the deeper intelligence of the true philosopher will understand that the possibilities of the universe are incalculable and that the wisest man is he who holds himself ready for the unexpected. To take an obvious example, who would undertake to say that the mysterious and universal outbreak of illness, recorded in your columns this very morning as having broken out among the indigenous races of Sumatra, has no connection with some cosmic change to which they may respond more quickly than the more complex peoples of Europe? I throw out the idea for what it is worth. To assert it is, in the present stage, as unprofitable as to deny it, but it is an unimaginative numbskull who is too dense to perceive that it is well within the bounds of scientific possibility.

> *Yours faithfully,*
> *George Edward Challenger*
> *The Briars, Rotherfield*

'It's a fine, steemulating letter,' said McArdle thoughtfully, fitting a cigarette into the long glass tube which he used as a holder. 'What's your opeenion of it, Mr Malone?'

I had to confess my total and humiliating ignorance of the subject at issue. What, for example, were Fraunhofer's lines? McArdle had just been studying the matter with the aid of our tame scientist at the office, and he picked from his desk two of those many-coloured spectral bands which bear a general resemblance to the hat-ribbons of some young and ambitious cricket club. He pointed out to me that there were certain black lines which formed crossbars upon the series of brilliant colours extending from the red at one end through gradations of orange, yellow, green, blue, and indigo to the violet at the other.

'Those dark bands are Fraunhofer's lines,' said he. 'The colours are just light itself. Every light, if you can split it up with a prism, gives the same colours. They tell us nothing. It is the lines that count, because they vary according to what it may be that produces the light. It is these lines that have been blurred instead of clear this last week, and all the astronomers have been quarrelling over the reason. Here's a photograph of the blurred lines for our issue tomorrow. The public have taken no interest in the matter up to now, but this letter of Challenger's in *The Times* will make them wake up, I'm thinking.'

'And this about Sumatra?'

'Well, it's a long cry from a blurred line in a spectrum to a sick person in Sumatra. And yet the chiel has shown us once before that he knows what he's talking about. There is some queer illness down yonder, that's beyond all doubt, and today there's a cable just come in from Singapore that the lighthouses are out of action in the Straits of Sudan, and two ships on the beach in consequence. Anyhow, it's good enough for you to interview Challenger upon. If you get anything definite, let us have a column by Monday.'

I was coming out from the news editor's room, turning over my new mission in my mind, when I heard my name called from the waiting room below. It was a telegraph boy with a wire which had been forwarded from my lodgings at Streatham. The message was from the very man we had been discussing, and ran thus:–

Malone, 17, Hill Street, Streatham. – Bring oxygen. – Challenger.

'Bring oxygen!' The Professor, as I remembered him, had an elephantine sense of humour capable of the most clumsy and unwieldly gambollings. Was this one of those jokes which used to reduce him to uproarious laughter, when his eyes would disappear and he was all gaping mouth and wagging beard, supremely indifferent to the gravity of all around him? I turned the words over, but could make nothing even remotely jocose out of them. Then surely it was a concise order – though a very strange one. He was the last man in the world whose deliberate command I should care to disobey. Possibly some chemical experiment was afoot; possibly – Well, it was no business of mine to speculate upon why he wanted it. I must get it. There was nearly an hour before I should catch the train at Victoria.

I took a taxi, and having ascertained the address from the telephone book, I made for the Oxygen Tube Supply Company in Oxford Street.

As I alighted on the pavement at my destination, two youths emerged from the door of the establishment carrying an iron cylinder, which, with some trouble, they hoisted into a waiting motor car. An elderly man was at their heels scolding and directing in a creaky, sardonic voice. He turned towards me. There was no mistaking those austere features and that goatee beard. It was my old cross-grained companion, Professor Summerlee.

'What!' he cried. 'Don't tell me that *you* have had one of these preposterous telegrams for oxygen?'

I exhibited it.

'Well, well! I have had one too, and, as you see, very much against the grain, I have acted upon it. Our good friend is as impossible as ever. The need for oxygen could not have been so urgent that he must desert the usual means of supply and encroach upon the time of those who are really busier than himself. Why could he not order it direct?'

I could only suggest that he probably wanted it at once.

'Or thought he did, which is quite another matter. But it is superfluous now for you to purchase any, since I have this considerable supply.'

'Still, for some reason he seems to wish that I should bring oxygen too. It will be safer to do exactly what he tells me.'

Accordingly, in spite of many grumbles and remonstrances from Summerlee, I ordered an additional tube, which was placed with the other in his motor car, for he had offered me a lift to Victoria.

I turned away to pay off my taxi, the driver of which was very cantankerous and abusive over his fare. As I came back to Professor Summerlee, he was having a furious altercation with the men who had carried down the oxygen, his little white goat's beard jerking with indignation. One of the fellows called him, I remember, 'a silly old bleached cockatoo,' which so enraged his chauffeur that he bounded out of his seat to take the part of his insulted master, and it was all we could do to prevent a riot in the street.

These little things may seem trivial to relate, and passed as mere incidents at the time. It is only now, as I look back, that I see their relation to the whole story which I have to unfold.

The chauffeur must, as it seemed to me, have been a novice or else have lost his nerve in this disturbance, for he drove vilely on the way to the station. Twice we nearly had collisions with other equally erratic vehicles, and I remember remarking to Summerlee that the standard of driving in London had very much declined. Once we brushed the very edge of a great crowd which was watching a fight at the corner of the Mall. The people, who were much excited, raised cries of anger at the clumsy driving, and one fellow sprang upon the step and waved a stick above our heads. I pushed him off, but we were glad when we had got clear of them and safe out of the park. These little events, coming one after the other, left me very jangled in my nerves, and I could see from my companion's petulant manner that his own patience had got to a low ebb.

But our good humour was restored when we saw Lord John Roxton waiting for us upon the platform, his tall, thin figure clad in a yellow tweed shooting suit. His keen face, with those unforgettable eyes, so fierce and yet so humorous, flushed with pleasure at the sight of us. His ruddy hair was shot with grey, and the furrows upon his brow had been cut a little deeper by Time's chisel, but in all else he was the Lord John who had been our good comrade in the past.

'Hullo, Herr Professor! Hullo, young fella!' he shouted as he came toward us.

He roared with amusement when he saw the oxygen cylinders upon the porter's trolly behind us.

'So you've got them too!' he cried. 'Mine is in the van. Whatever can the old dear be after?'

'Have you seen his letter in *The Times*?' I asked.

'What was it?'

'Stuff and nonsense!' said Summerlee harshly.

'Well, it's at the bottom of this oxygen business, or I am mistaken,' said I.

'Stuff and nonsense!' cried Summerlee again with quite unnecessary violence.

We had all got into a first-class smoker, and he had already lit the short and charred old brier pipe which seemed to singe the end of his long, aggressive nose.

'Friend Challenger is a clever man,' said he with great vehemence. 'No one can deny it. It's a fool that denies it. Look at his hat. There's a sixty-ounce brain inside it – a big engine, running smooth, and turning out clean work. Show me the engine house and I'll tell you the size of the engine. But he is a born charlatan – you've heard me tell him so to his face – a born charlatan, with a kind of dramatic trick of jumping into the limelight. Things are quiet, so friend Challenger sees a chance to set the public talking about him. You don't imagine that he seriously believes all this nonsense about a change in the ether and a danger to the human race? Was ever such a cock-and-bull story in this life?'

He sat like an old white raven, croaking and shaking with sardonic laughter.

A wave of anger passed through me as I listened to Summerlee. It was disgraceful that he should speak thus of the leader who had been the source of all our fame and given us such an experience as no men have ever enjoyed. I had opened my mouth to utter some hot retort, when Lord John got before me.

'You had a scrap once before with old man Challenger,' said he sternly, 'and you were down and out inside ten seconds. It seems to me, Professor Summerlee, he's beyond your class, and the best you can do with him is to walk wide and leave him alone.'

'Besides,' said I, 'he has been a good friend to every one of us. Whatever his faults may be, he is as straight as a line, and I don't believe he ever speaks evil of his comrades behind their backs.'

'Well said, young fellah-my-lad,' said Lord John Roxton. Then, with a kindly smile, he slapped Professor Summerlee upon his shoulder. 'Come, Herr Professor, we're not goin' to quarrel at this time of day. We've seen too much together. But keep off the grass when you get near Challenger, for this young fellah and I have a bit of a weakness for the old dear.'

But Summerlee was in no humour for compromise. His face was screwed up in rigid disapproval, and thick curls of angry smoke rolled up from his pipe.

'As to you, Lord John Roxton,' he creaked, 'your opinion upon a matter of science is of as much value in my eyes as my views upon a new type of shotgun would be in yours. I have my own judgment, sir, and I use it in my own way. Because it has misled me once, is that any reason why I should accept without criticism anything, however far-fetched, which this man may care to put forward? Are we to have a Pope of science, with infallible decrees laid down *ex cathedra*, and accepted without question by the poor humble public? I tell you, sir, that I have a brain of my own and that I should feel myself to be a snob and a slave if I did not use it. If it pleases you to believe this rigmarole about ether and Fraunhofer's lines upon the spectrum, do so by all means, but do not ask one who is older and wiser than yourself to share in your folly. Is it not evident that if the ether were affected to the degree which he maintains, and if it were obnoxious to human health, the result of it would already be apparent upon ourselves?' Here he laughed with uproarious triumph over his own argument. 'Yes, sir, we should already be very far from our normal selves, and instead of sitting quietly discussing scientific problems in a railway train we should be showing actual symptoms of the poison which was working within us. Where do we see any signs of this poisonous cosmic disturbance? Answer me that, sir! Answer me that! Come, come, no evasion! I pin you to an answer!'

I felt more and more angry. There was something very irritating and aggressive in Summerlee's demeanour.

'I think that if you knew more about the facts you might be less positive in your opinion,' said I.

Summerlee took his pipe from his mouth and fixed me with a stony stare.

'Pray what do you mean, sir, by that somewhat impertinent-observation?'

'I mean that when I was leaving the office the news editor told me that a telegram had come in confirming the general illness of the Sumatra natives, and adding that the lights had not been lit in the Straits of Sunda.'

'Really, there should be some limits to human folly!' cried Summerlee in a positive fury. 'Is it possible that you do not realise that ether, if for a moment we adopt Challenger's preposterous supposition, is a universal substance which is the same here as at the other side of the world? Do you for an instant suppose that there is an English ether and a Sumatran ether? Perhaps you imagine that the ether of Kent is in some way superior to the ether of Surrey, through which this train is now bearing us. There really are no bounds to the credulity and ignorance of the average layman. Is it conceivable that the ether in Sumatra should be so deadly as to cause total insensibility at the very time when the ether here has had no appreciable effect upon us whatever? Personally, I can truly say that I never felt stronger in body or better balanced in mind in my life.'

'That may be. I don't profess to be a scientific man,' said I, 'though I have heard somewhere that the science of one generation is usually the fallacy of the next. But it does not take much common sense to see that, as we seem to know so little about ether, it might be affected by some local conditions in various parts of the world and might show an effect over there which would only develop later with us.'

'With "might" and "may" you can prove anything,' cried Summerlee furiously. 'Pigs may fly. Yes, sir, pigs *may* fly – but they don't. It is not worth arguing with you. Challenger has filled you with his nonsense and you are both incapable of reason. I had as soon lay arguments before those railway cushions.'

'I must say, Professor Summerlee, that your manners do not seem to have improved since I last had the pleasure of meetin' you,' said Lord John severely.

'You lordlings are not accustomed to hear the truth,' Summerlee answered with a bitter smile. 'It comes as a bit of a shock, does it not, when someone makes you realise that your title leaves you none the less a very ignorant man?'

'Upon my word, sir,' said Lord John, very stern and rigid, 'if you were a younger man you would not dare to speak to me in so offensive a fashion.'

Summerlee thrust out his chin, with its little wagging tuft of goatee beard.

'I would have you know, sir, that, young or old, there has never been a time in my life when I was afraid to speak my mind to an ignorant coxcomb – yes, sir, an ignorant coxcomb, if you had as many titles as slaves could invent and fools could adopt.'

For a moment Lord John's eyes blazed, and then, with a tremendous effort, he mastered his anger and leaned back in his seat with arms folded and a bitter smile upon his face. To me all this was dreadful and deplorable. Like a wave, the memory of the past swept over me, the good comradeship, the happy, adventurous days – all that we had suffered and worked for and won. That it should have come to this – to insults and abuse! Suddenly I was sobbing – sobbing in loud, gulping, uncontrollable sobs which refused to be concealed. My companions looked at me in surprise. I covered my face with my hands.

'It's all right,' said I. 'Only – only it *is* such a pity!'

'You're ill, young fellah, that's what's amiss with you,' said Lord John. 'I thought you were queer from the first.'

'Your habits, sir, have not mended in these three years,' said Summerlee, shaking his head. 'I also did not fail to observe your strange manner the moment we met. You need not waste your sympathy, Lord John. These tears are purely alcoholic. The man has been drinking. By the way, Lord John, I called you a coxcomb just now, which was, perhaps, unduly severe. But the word reminds me of a small accomplishment, trivial but amusing, which I used to possess. You know me as the austere man of science. Can you believe that I once had a well-deserved reputation in several nurseries as a farmyard imitator? Perhaps I can help you to pass the time in a pleasant way. Would it amuse you to hear me crow like a cock?'

'No, sir,' said Lord John, who was still greatly offended, 'it would *not* amuse me.'

'My imitation of the clucking hen who had just laid an egg was also considered rather above the average. Might I venture?'

'No, sir, no – certainly not.'

But, in spite of this earnest prohibition, Professor Summerlee laid down his pipe and for the rest of our journey he entertained – or failed to entertain – us by a succession of bird and animal cries which seemed so absurd that my tears were suddenly changed into boisterous laughter, which must have become quite hysterical as I sat opposite this grave Professor and saw him – or rather heard him – in the character of the uproarious rooster or the puppy whose tail had been trodden upon. Once Lord John passed across his newspaper, upon the margin of which he had written in pencil, 'Poor devil! Mad as a hatter.' No doubt it was very eccentric, and yet the performance struck me as extraordinarily clever and amusing.

Whilst this was going on, Lord John leaned forward and told me some interminable story about a buffalo and an Indian rajah which seemed to me to have neither beginning nor end. Professor Summerlee had just begun to chirrup like a canary, and Lord John to get to the climax of his story, when the train drew up at Jarvis Brook, which had been given us as the station for Rotherfield.

And there was Challenger to meet us. His appearance was glorious. Not all the turkey-cocks in creation could match the slow, high-stepping dignity with which he paraded his own railway station and the benignant smile of condescending encouragement with which he regarded everybody around him. If he had changed in anything since the days of old, it was that his points had become accentuated. The huge head and broad sweep of forehead, with its plastered lock of black hair, seemed even greater than before. His black beard poured forward in a more impressive cascade, and his clear grey eyes, with their insolent and sardonic eyelids, were even more masterful than of yore.

He gave me the amused handshake and encouraging smile which the headmaster bestows upon the small boy, and, having greeted the others and helped to collect their bags and their cylinders of oxygen, he stowed us and them away in a large motor car which was driven by the same impassive Austin, the man of few words, whom I had seen in the character of butler upon the occasion of my first eventful visit to the Professor. Our journey led us up a winding hill through beautiful country.

I sat in front with the chauffeur, but behind me my three comrades seemed to me to be all talking together. Lord John was still struggling with his buffalo story, so far as I could make out, while once again I heard, as of old, the deep rumble of Challenger and the insistent accents of Summerlee as their brains locked in high and fierce scientific debate. Suddenly Austin slanted his mahogany face toward me without taking his eyes from his steering wheel.

'I'm under notice,' said he.

'Dear me!' said I.

Everything seemed strange today. Everyone said queer, un-expected things. It was like a dream.

'It's forty-seven times,' said Austin reflectively.

'When do you go?' I asked, for want of some better observation.

'I don't go,' said Austin.

The conversation seemed to have ended there, but presently he came back to it.

'If I was to go, who would look after 'im?' He jerked his head toward his master. 'Who would 'e get to serve 'im?'

'Someone else,' I suggested, lamely.

'Not 'e. No one would stay a week. If I was to go, that 'ouse would run down like a watch with the mainspring out. I'm telling you because you're 'is friend, and you ought to know. If I was to take 'im at 'is word – but there, I wouldn't have the 'eart. 'E and the missus would be like two babes left out in a bundle. I'm just everything. And then 'e goes and gives me notice.'

'Why would no one stay?' I asked.

'Well, they wouldn't make allowances, same as I do. 'E's a very clever man, the master – so clever that 'e's clean barmy sometimes. I've seen 'im right off 'is onion, and no error. Well, look what 'e did this morning.'

'What did he do?'

Austin bent over to me.

''E bit the 'ousekeeper,' said he in a hoarse whisper.

'Bit her?'

'Yes, sir. Bit 'er on the leg. I saw 'er with my own eyes startin' a marathon from the 'all door.'

'Good gracious!'

'So you'd say, sir, if you could see some of the goings on. 'E don't make friends with the neighbours. There's some of them thinks that when 'e was up among those monsters you wrote about, it was just "'Ome, Sweet 'Ome' for the master, and 'e was never in fitter company. That's what *they* say. But I've served 'im ten years, and I'm fond of 'im, and, mind you, 'e's a great man, when all's said an' done, and it's an honour to serve 'im. But 'e does try one cruel at times. Now look at that, sir. That ain't what you might call old-fashioned 'ospitality, is it now? Just you read it for yourself.'

The car on its lowest speed had ground its way up a steep, curving ascent. At the corner a noticeboard peered over a well-clipped hedge. As Austin said, it was not difficult to read, for the words were few and arresting:–

WARNING.

Visitors, Pressmen, and Mendicants are not encouraged.

– G.E. Challenger

'No, it's not what you might call 'earty,' said Austin, shaking his head and glancing up at the deplorable placard. 'It wouldn't look well in a Christmas card. I beg your pardon, sir, for I haven't spoke as much as this for many a long year, but today my feelings seem to 'ave got the better of me. 'E can sack me till 'e's blue in the face, but I ain't going, and that's flat. I'm 'is man and 'e's my master, and so it will be, I expect, to the end of the chapter.'

We had passed between the white posts of a gate and up a curving drive, lined with rhododendron bushes. Beyond stood a low brick house, picked out with white woodwork, very comfortable and pretty. Mrs Challenger, a small, dainty, smiling figure, stood in the open doorway to welcome us.

'Well, my dear,' said Challenger, bustling out of the car, 'here are our visitors. It is something new for us to have visitors, is it not? No love lost between us and our neighbours, is there? If they could get rat poison into our baker's cart, I expect it would be there.'

'It's dreadful – dreadful!' cried the lady, between laughter and tears. 'George is always quarrelling with everyone. We haven't a friend on the countryside.'

'It enables me to concentrate my attention upon my incomparable wife,' said Challenger, passing his short, thick arm round her waist. Picture a gorilla and a gazelle, and you have the pair of them. 'Come, come, these gentlemen are tired from the journey, and luncheon should be ready. Has Sarah returned?'

The lady shook her head ruefully, and the Professor laughed loudly and stroked his beard in his masterful fashion.

'Austin,' he cried, 'when you have put up the car you will kindly help your mistress to lay the lunch. Now, gentlemen, will you please step into my study, for there are one or two very urgent things which I am anxious to say to you.'

2

The Tide of Death

As we crossed the hall the telephone bell rang, and we were the involuntary auditors of Professor Challenger's end of the ensuing dialogue. I say 'we', but no one within a hundred yards could have failed to hear the booming of that monstrous voice, which reverberated through the house. His answers lingered in my mind.

'Yes, yes, of course, it is I... Yes, certainly, *the* Professor Challenger, the famous Professor, who else?... Of course, every word of it, otherwise I should not have written it... I shouldn't be surprised... There is every indication of it...Within a day or so at the furthest.... Well, I can't help that, can I?... Very unpleasant, no doubt, but I rather fancy it will affect more important people than you. There is no use whining about it... No, I couldn't possibly. You must take your chance... That's enough, sir. Nonsense! I have something more important to do than to listen to such twaddle.'

He shut off with a crash and led us upstairs into a large airy apartment which formed his study. On the great mahogany desk seven or eight unopened telegrams were lying.

'Really,' he said as he gathered them up, 'I begin to think that it would save my correspondents' money if I were to adopt a telegraphic address. Possibly "Noah, Rotherfield", would be the most appropriate.'

As usual when he made an obscure joke, he leaned against the desk and bellowed in a paroxysm of laughter, his hands shaking so that he could hardly open the envelopes.

'Noah! Noah!' he gasped, with a face of beetroot, while Lord John and I smiled in sympathy and Summerlee, like a dyspeptic goat, wagged his head in sardonic disagreement.

Finally Challenger, still rumbling and exploding, began to open his telegrams. The three of us stood in the bow window and occupied ourselves in admiring the magnificent view.

It was certainly worth looking at. The road in its gentle curves had really brought us to a considerable elevation – seven hundred feet, as we afterwards discovered. Challenger's house was on the very edge of the hill, and from its southern face, in which was the study window, one looked across the vast stretch of the weald to where the gentle curves of the South Downs formed an undulating horizon. In a cleft of the hills a haze of smoke marked the position of Lewes. Immediately at our feet there lay a rolling plain of heather, with the long, vivid green stretches of the Crowborough golf course, all dotted with the players. A little to the south, through an opening in the woods, we could see a section of the main line from London to Brighton. In the immediate foreground, under our very noses, was a small enclosed yard, in which stood the car which had brought us from the station.

An ejaculation from Challenger caused us to turn. He had read his telegrams and had arranged them in a little method-ical pile upon his desk. His broad, rugged face, or as much of it as was visible over the matted beard, was still deeply flushed, and he seemed to be under the influence of some strong excite-ment.

'Well, gentlemen,' he said, in a voice as if he was addressing a public meeting, 'this is indeed an interesting reunion, and it takes place under extraordinary – I may say unprecedented – circumstances. May I ask if you have observed anything upon your journey from town?'

'The only thing which I observed,' said Summerlee with a sour smile, 'was that our young friend here has not improved in his manners during the years that have passed. I am sorry to state that I have had to seriously complain of his conduct in the train, and I should be wanting in frankness if I did not say that it has left a most unpleasant impression in my mind.'

'Well, well, we all get a bit prosy sometimes,' said Lord John. 'The young fellah meant no real harm. After all, he's an International, so if he takes half an hour to describe a game of football he has more right to do it than most folk.'

'Half an hour to describe a game!' I cried indignantly. 'Why, it was you that took half an hour with some longwinded story about a buffalo. Professor Summerlee will be my witness.'

'I can hardly judge which of you was the most utterly wearisome,' said Summerlee. 'I declare to you, Challenger, that I never wish to hear of football or of buffaloes so long as I live.'

'I have never said one word today about football,' I protested.

Lord John gave a shrill whistle, and Summerlee shook his head sadly.

'So early in the day too,' said he. 'It is indeed deplorable. As I sat there in sad but thoughtful silence –'

'In silence!' cried Lord John. 'Why, you were doin' a music-hall turn of imitations all the way – more like a runaway gramophone than a man.'

Summerlee drew himself up in bitter protest.

'You are pleased to be facetious, Lord John,' said he, with a face of vinegar.

'Why, dash it all, this is clear madness,' cried Lord John. 'Each of us seems to know what the others did and none of us knows what he did himself. Let's put it all together from the first. We got into a first-class smoker, that's clear, ain't it? Then we began to quarrel over friend Challenger's letter in *The Times*.'

'Oh, you did, did you?' rumbled our host, his eyelids beginning to droop.

'You said, Summerlee, that there was no possible truth in his contention.'

'Dear me!' said Challenger, puffing out his chest and stroking his beard. 'No possible truth! I seem to have heard the words before. And may I ask with what arguments the great and famous Professor Summerlee proceeded to demolish the humble individual who had ventured to express an opinion upon a matter of scientific possibility? Perhaps before he exterminates that unfortunate nonentity he will condescend to give some reasons for the adverse views which he has formed.'

He bowed and shrugged and spread open his hands as he spoke with his elaborate and elephantine sarcasm.

'The reason was simple enough,' said the dogged Summerlee. 'I contended that if the ether surrounding the earth was so toxic in one quarter that it produced dangerous symptoms, it was hardly likely that we three in the railway carriage should be entirely unaffected.'

The explanation only brought uproarious merriment from Challenger. He laughed until everything in the room seemed to rattle and quiver.

'Our worthy Summerlee is, not for the first time, somewhat out of touch with the facts of the situation,' said he at last, mopping his heated brow. 'Now, gentlemen, I cannot make my point better than by detailing to you what I have myself done this morning. You will the more easily condone any mental aberration upon your own part when you realise that even I have had moments when my balance has been disturbed. We have had for some years in this household a housekeeper – one Sarah, with whose second name I have never attempted to burden my memory. She is a woman of a severe and forbidding aspect, prim and demure in her bearing, very impassive in her nature, and never known within our experience to show signs of any emotion. As I sat alone at my breakfast – Mrs Challenger is in the habit of keeping her room of a morning – it suddenly entered my head that it would be entertaining and instructive to see whether I could find any limits to this woman's imperturbability. I devised a simple but effective experiment. Having upset a small vase of flowers which stood in the centre of the cloth, I rang the bell and slipped under the table. She entered and, seeing the room empty, imagined that I had withdrawn to the study. As I had expected, she approached and leaned over the table to replace the vase. I had a vision of a cotton stocking and an elastic-sided boot. Protruding my head, I sank my teeth into the calf of her leg. The experiment was successful beyond belief. For some moments she stood paralysed, staring down at my head. Then with a shriek she tore herself free and rushed from the room. I pursued her with some thoughts of an explanation, but she flew down the drive, and some minutes afterwards I was able to pick her out with my field-glasses travelling very rapidly in a south-westerly direction. I tell you the anecdote for what it is worth. I drop it into your brains and await its germination. Is it illuminative? Has it conveyed anything to your minds? What do *you* think of it, Lord John?'

Lord John shook his head gravely.

'You'll be gettin' into serious trouble some of these days if you don't put a brake on,' said he.

'Perhaps you have some observation to make, Summerlee?'

'You should drop all work instantly, Challenger, and take three months in a German watering place,' said he.

'Profound! Profound!' cried Challenger. 'Now, my young friend, is it possible that wisdom may come from you where your seniors have so signally failed?'

And it did. I say it with all modesty, but it did. Of course, it all seems obvious enough to you who know what occurred, but it was not so very clear when everything was new. But it came on me suddenly with the full force of absolute conviction.

'Poison!' I cried.

Then, even as I said the word, my mind flashed back over the whole morning's experiences, past Lord John with his buffalo, past my own hysterical tears, past the outrageous conduct of Professor Summerlee, to the queer happenings in London, the row in the park, the driving of the chauffeur, the quarrel at the oxygen warehouse. Everything fitted suddenly into its place.

'Of course,' I cried again. 'It is poison. We are all poisoned.'

'Exactly,' said Challenger, rubbing his hands, 'we are all poisoned. Our planet has swum into the poison belt of ether, and is now flying deeper into it at the rate of some millions of miles a minute. Our young friend has expressed the cause of all our troubles and perplexities in a single word, "poison".'

We looked at each other in amazed silence. No comment seemed to meet the situation.

'There is a mental inhibition by which such symptoms can be checked and controlled,' said Challenger. 'I cannot expect to find it developed in all of you to the same point which it has reached in me, for I suppose that the strength of our different mental processes bears some proportion to each other. But no doubt it is appreciable even in our young friend here. After the little outburst of high spirits which so alarmed my domestic I sat down and reasoned with myself. I put it to myself that I had never before felt impelled to bite any of my household. The impulse had then been an abnormal one. In an instant I perceived the truth. My pulse upon examination was ten beats above the usual, and my reflexes were increased. I called upon my higher and saner self, the real G.E.C., seated serene and impregnable behind all mere molecular disturbance. I summoned him, I say, to watch the foolish mental tricks which the poison would play. I found that I was indeed the master. I could recognise and control a disordered mind. It was a remarkable exhibition of the victory of mind over matter, for it was a victory over that particular form of matter which is most intimately connected with mind. I might almost say that mind was at fault and that personality controlled it. Thus, when my wife came downstairs and I was impelled to slip behind the door and alarm her by some wild cry as she entered, I was able to stifle the impulse and to greet her with dignity and restraint. An over-powering desire to quack like a duck was met and mastered in the same fashion.

'Later, when I descended to order the car and found Austin bending over it absorbed in repairs, I controlled my open hand even after I had lifted it, and refrained from giving him an experience which would possibly have caused him to follow in the steps of the housekeeper. On the contrary, I touched him on the shoulder and ordered the car to be at the door in time to meet your train. At the present instant I am most forcibly tempted to take Professor Summerlee by that silly old beard of his, and to shake his head violently backwards and forwards. And yet, as you see, I am perfectly restrained. Let me commend my example to you.'

'I'll look out for that buffalo,' said Lord John.

'And I for the football match.'

'It may be that you are right, Challenger,' said Summerlee in a chastened voice. 'I am willing to admit that my turn of mind is critical rather than constructive, and that I am not a ready convert to any new theory, especially when it happens to be so unusual and fantastic as this one. However, as I cast my mind back over the events of the morning, and as I reconsider the fatuous conduct of my companions, I find it easy to believe that some poison of an exciting kind was responsible for their symptoms.'

Challenger slapped his colleague good-humouredly upon the shoulder. 'We progress,' said he. 'Decidedly we progress.'

'And pray, sir,' asked Summerlee humbly, 'what is your opinion as to the present outlook?'

'With your permission I will say a few words upon that subject.' He seated himself upon his desk, his short, stumpy legs swinging in front of him. 'We are assisting at a tremendous and awful function. It is, in my opinion, the end of the world.'

The end of the world! Our eyes turned to the great bow-window and we looked out at the summer beauty of the country-side, the long slopes of heather, the great country houses, the cosy farms, the pleasure seekers upon the links. The end of the world! One had often heard the words, but the idea that they could ever have an immediate practical significance, that it should not be at some vague date, but now, today, that was a tremendous, a staggering thought. We were all struck solemn and waited in silence for Challenger to continue. His overpowering presence and appearance lent such force to the solemnity of his words that for a moment all the crudities and absurdities of the man vanished, and he loomed before us as something majestic and beyond the range of ordinary humanity. Then to me, at least, there came back the cheering recollection of how twice since we had entered the room he had roared with laughter. Surely, I thought, there are limits to mental detachment. The crisis cannot be so great or so pressing after all.

'You will conceive a bunch of grapes,' said he, 'which are covered by some infinitesimal but noxious bacillus. The gardener passes it through a disinfecting medium. It may be that he desires his grapes to be cleaner. It may be that he needs space to breed some fresh bacillus less noxious than the last. He dips it into the poison and they are gone. Our Gardener is, in my opinion, about to dip the solar system, and the human bacillus, the little mortal vibrio which twisted and wriggled upon the outer rind of the earth, will in an instant be sterilised out of existence.'

Again there was silence. It was broken by the high trill of the telephone bell.

'There is one of our bacilli squeaking for help,' said he with a grim smile. 'They are beginning to realise that their continued existence is not really one of the necessities of the universe.'

He was gone from the room for a minute or two. I remember that none of us spoke in his absence. The situation seemed beyond all words or comments.

'The medical officer of health for Brighton,' said he when he returned. 'The symptoms are for some reason developing more rapidly upon the sea level. Our seven hundred feet of elevation give us an advantage. Folk seem to have learned that I am the first authority upon the question. No doubt it comes from my letter in *The Times*. That was the mayor of a provincial town with whom I talked when we first arrived. You may have heard me upon the telephone. He seemed to put an entirely inflated value upon his own life. I helped him to readjust his ideas.'

Summerlee had risen and was standing by the window. His thin, bony hands were trembling with his emotion.

'Challenger,' said he earnestly, 'this thing is too serious for mere futile argument. Do not suppose that I desire to irritate you by any question I may ask. But I put it to you whether there may not be some fallacy in your information or in your reasoning. There is the sun shining as brightly as ever in a blue sky. There are the heather and the flowers and the birds. There are the folk enjoying themselves upon the golf links, and the labourers yonder cutting the corn. You tell us that they and we may be upon the very brink of destruction – that this sunlit day may be that day of doom which the human race has so long awaited. So far as we know, you found this tremendous judgment upon what? Upon some abnormal lines in a spectrum – upon rumours from Sumatra – upon some curious personal excitement which we have discerned in each other. This latter symptom is not so marked but that you and we could, by a deliberate effort, control it. You need not stand on ceremony with us, Challenger. We have all faced death together before now. Speak out, and let us know exactly where we stand, and what, in your opinion, are our prospects for our future.'

It was a brave, good speech, a speech from that staunch and strong spirit which lay behind all the acidities and angularities of the old zoologist. Lord John rose and shook him by the hand.

'My sentiment to a tick,' said he. 'Now, Challenger, it's up to you to tell us where we are. We ain't nervous folk, as you know well; but when it comes to makin' a weekend visit and findin' you've run full butt into the Day of Judgment, it wants a bit of explainin'. What's the danger, and how much of it is there, and what are we goin' to do to meet it?'

He stood, tall and strong, in the sunshine at the window, with his brown hand upon the shoulder of Summerlee. I was lying back in an armchair, an extinguished cigarette between my lips, in that sort of half-dazed state in which impressions become exceedingly distinct. It may have been a new phase of the poisoning, but the delirious promptings had all passed away and were succeeded by an exceedingly languid and, at the same time, perceptive state of mind. I was a spectator. It did not seem to be any personal concern of mine. But here were three strong men at a great crisis, and it was fascinating to observe them. Challenger bent his heavy brows and stroked his beard before he answered. One could see that he was very carefully weighing his words.

'What was the last news when you left London?' he asked.

'I was at the *Gazette* office about ten,' said I. 'There was a Reuter just come in from Singapore to the effect that the sickness seemed to be universal in Sumatra and that the lighthouses had not been lit in consequence.'

'Events have been moving somewhat rapidly since then,' said Challenger, picking up his pile of telegrams. 'I am in close touch both with the authorities and with the press, so that news is converging upon me from all parts. There is, in fact, a general and very insistent demand that I should come to London; but I see no good end to be served. From the accounts the poisonous effect begins with mental excitement; the rioting in Paris this morning is said to have been very violent, and the Welsh colliers are in a state of uproar. So far as the evidence to hand can be trusted, this stimulative stage, which varies much in races and in individuals, is succeeded by a certain exaltation and mental lucidity – I seem to discern some signs of it in our young friend here – which, after an appreciable interval, turns to coma, deepening rapidly into death. I fancy, so far as my toxicology carries me, that there are some vegetable nerve poisons –'

'Datura,' suggested Summerlee.

'Excellent!' cried Challenger. 'It would make for scientific precision if we named our toxic agent. Let it be daturon. To you, my dear Summerlee, belongs the honour – posthumous, alas, but none the less unique – of having given a name to the universal destroyer, the Great Gardener's disinfectant. The symptoms of daturon, then, may be taken to be such as I indicate. That it will involve the whole world and that no life can possibly remain behind seems to me to be certain, since ether is a universal medium. Up to now it has been capricious in the places which it has attacked, but the difference is only a matter of a few hours, and it is like an advancing tide which covers one strip of sand and then another, running hither and thither in irregular streams, until at last it has submerged it all. There are laws at work in connection with the action and distribution of daturon which would have been of deep interest had the time at our disposal permitted us to study them. So far as I can trace them' – here he glanced over his telegrams – 'the less developed races have been the first to respond to its influence. There are deplorable accounts from Africa, and the Australian aborigines appear to have been already exterminated. The Northern races have as yet shown greater resisting power than the Southern. This, you see, is dated from Marseilles at nine forty-five this morning. I give it to you verbatim:–

'*All night delirious excitement throughout Provence. Tumult of vine growers at Nîmes. Socialistic upheaval at Toulon. Sudden illness attended by coma attacked population this morning.* Peste foudroyant. *Great numbers of dead in the streets. Paralysis of business and universal chaos.*

'An hour later came the following, from the same source:–

'*We are threatened with utter extermination. Cathedrals and churches full to overflowing. The dead outnumber the living. It is inconceivable and horrible. Decease seems to be painless, but swift and inevitable.*

'There is a similar telegram from Paris, where the development is not yet as acute. India and Persia appear to be utterly wiped out. The Slavonic population of Austria is down, while the Teutonic has hardly been affected. Speaking generally, the dwellers upon the plains and upon the seashore seem, so far as my limited information goes, to have felt the effects more rapidly than those inland or on the heights. Even a little eleva-tion makes a considerable difference, and perhaps if there be a survivor of the human race, he will again be found upon the summit of some Ararat. Even our own little hill may presently prove to be a temporary island amid a sea of disaster. But at the present rate of advance a few short hours will submerge us all.'

Lord John Roxton wiped his brow.

'What beats me,' said he, 'is how you could sit there laughin' with that stack of telegrams under your hand. I've seen death as often as most folk, but universal death – it's awful!'

'As to the laughter,' said Challenger, 'you will bear in mind that, like yourselves, I have not been exempt from the stimu-lating cerebral effects of the etheric poison. But as to the horror with which universal death appears to inspire you, I would put it to you that it is somewhat exaggerated. If you were sent to sea alone in an open boat to some unknown destination, your heart might well sink within you. The isolation, the uncertainty, would oppress you. But if your voyage were made in a goodly ship, which bore within it all your relations and your friends, you would feel that, however uncertain your destination might still remain, you would at least have one common and simultaneous experience which would hold you to the end in the same close communion. A lonely death may be terrible, but a universal one, as painless as this would appear to be, is not, in my judgment, a matter for apprehension. Indeed, I could sympathise with the person who took the view that the horror lay in the idea of surviving when all that is learned, famous, and exalted had passed away.'

'What, then, do you propose to do?' asked Summerlee, who had for once nodded his assent to the reasoning of his brother scientist.

'To take our lunch,' said Challenger as the boom of a gong sounded through the house. 'We have a cook whose omelettes are only excelled by her cutlets. We can but trust that no cosmic disturbance has dulled her excellent abilities. My Scharzberger of '96 must also be rescued, so far as our earnest and united efforts can do it, from what would be a deplorable waste of a great vintage.' He levered his great bulk off the desk, upon which he had sat while he announced the doom of the planet. 'Come,' said he. 'If there is little time left, there is the more need that we should spend it in sober and reasonable enjoyment.'

And, indeed, it proved to be a very merry meal. It is true that we could not forget our awful situation. The full solemnity of the event loomed ever at the back of our minds and tempered our thoughts. But surely it is the soul which has never faced death which shies strongly from it at the end. To each of us men it had, for one great epoch in our lives, been a familiar presence.

As to the lady, she leaned upon the strong guidance of her mighty husband and was well content to go whither his path might lead. The future was our fate. The present was our own. We passed it in goodly comradeship and gentle merriment. Our minds were, as I have said, singularly lucid. Even I struck sparks at times. As to Challenger, he was wonderful! Never have I so realised the elemental greatness of the man, the sweep and power of his understanding. Summerlee drew him on with his chorus of subacid criticism, while Lord John and I laughed at the contest and the lady, her hand upon his sleeve, controlled the bellowings of the philosopher. Life, death, fate, the destiny of man – these were the stupendous subjects of that memorable hour, made vital by the fact that as the meal progressed strange, sudden exaltations in my mind and tinglings in my limbs proclaimed that the invisible tide of death was slowly and gently rising around us. Once I saw Lord John put his hand suddenly to his eyes, and once Summerlee dropped back for an instant in his chair. Each breath we breathed was charged with strange forces. And yet our minds were happy and at ease. Presently Austin laid the cigarettes upon the table and was about to withdraw.

'Austin!' said his master.

'Yes, sir?'

'I thank you for your faithful service.' A smile stole over the servant's gnarled face.

'I've done my duty, sir.'

'I'm expecting the end of the world today, Austin.'

'Yes, sir. What time, sir?'

'I can't say, Austin. Before evening.'

'Very good, sir.'

The taciturn Austin saluted and withdrew. Challenger lit a cigarette, and, drawing his chair closer to his wife's, he took her hand in his.

'You know how matters stand, dear,' said he. 'I have explained it also to our friends here. You're not afraid are you?'

'It won't be painful, George?'

'No more than laughing gas at the dentist's. Every time you have had it you have practically died.'

'But that is a pleasant sensation.'

'So may death be. The worn-out bodily machine can't record its impression, but we know the mental pleasure which lies in a dream or a trance. Nature may build a beautiful door and hang it with many a gauzy and shimmering curtain to make an entrance to the new life for our wondering souls. In all my probings of the actual, I have always found wisdom and kindness at the core; and if ever the frightened mortal needs tenderness, it is surely as he makes the passage perilous from life to life. No, Summerlee, I will have none of your materialism, for I, at least, am too great a thing to end in mere physical constituents, a packet of salts and three bucketfuls of water. Here – here' – and he beat his great head with his huge, hairy fist – 'there is something which uses matter, but is not of it – something which might destroy death, but which death can never destroy.'

'Talkin' of death,' said Lord John. 'I'm a Christian of sorts, but it seems to me there was somethin' mighty natural in those ancestors of ours who were buried with their axes and bows and arrows and the like, same as if they were livin' on just the same as they used to. I don't know,' he added, looking round the table in a shamefaced way, 'that I wouldn't feel more homely myself if I was put away with my old .450 Express and the fowlin'-piece, the shorter one with the rubbered stock, and a clip or two of cartridges – just a fool's fancy, of course, but there it is. How does it strike you, Herr Professor?'

'Well,' said Summerlee, 'since you ask my opinion, it strikes me as an indefensible throwback to the Stone Age or before it. I'm of the twentieth century myself, and would wish to die like a reasonable civilised man. I don't know that I am more afraid of death than the rest of you, for I am an oldish man, and, come what may, I can't have very much longer to live; but it is all against my nature to sit waiting without a struggle like a sheep for the butcher. Is it quite certain, Challenger, that there is nothing we can do?'

'To save us – nothing,' said Challenger. 'To prolong our lives a few hours and thus to see the evolution of this mighty tragedy before we are actually involved in it – that may prove to be within my powers. I have taken certain steps –'

'The oxygen?'

'Exactly. The oxygen.'

'But what can oxygen effect in the face of a poisoning of the ether? There is not a greater difference in quality between a brick-bat and a gas than there is between oxygen and ether. They are different planes of matter. They cannot impinge upon one another. Come, Challenger, you could not defend such a proposition.'

'My good Summerlee, this etheric poison is most certainly influenced by material agents. We see it in the methods and distribution of the outbreak. We should not *a priori* have expected it, but it is undoubtedly a fact. Hence I am strongly of the opinion that a gas like oxygen, which increases the vitality and the resisting power of the body, would be extremely likely to delay the action of what you have so happily named the daturon. It may be that I am mistaken, but I have every confidence in the correctness of my reasoning.'

'Well,' said Lord John, 'if we've got to sit suckin' at those tubes like so many babies with their bottles, I'm not takin' any.'

'There will be no need for that,' Challenger answered. 'We have made arrangements – it is to my wife that you chiefly owe it – that her boudoir shall be made as airtight as is practicable. With matting and varnished paper –'

'Good heavens, Challenger, you don't suppose you can keep out ether with varnished paper?'

'Really, my worthy friend, you are a trifle perverse in missing the point. It is not to keep out the ether that we have gone to such trouble. It is to keep in the oxygen. I trust that if we can ensure an atmosphere hyperoxygenated to a certain point, we may be able to retain our senses. I had two tubes of the gas and you have brought me three more. It is not much, but it is something.'

'How long will they last?'

'I have not an idea. We will not turn them on until our symptoms become unbearable. Then we shall dole the gas out as it is urgently needed. It may give us some hours, possibly even some days, on which we may look out upon a blasted world. Our own fate is delayed to that extent, and we will have the very singular experience, we five, of being, in all probability, the absolute rearguard of the human race upon its march into the unknown. Perhaps you will be kind enough now to give me a hand with the cylinders. It seems to me that the atmosphere already grows somewhat more oppressive.'

3

Submerged

The chamber which was destined to be the scene of our unforgettable experience was a charmingly feminine sitting room, some fourteen or sixteen feet square. At the end of it, divided by a curtain of red velvet, was a small apartment which formed the Professor's dressing room. This in turn opened into a large bedroom. The curtain was still hanging, but the boudoir and dressing room could be taken as one chamber for the purposes of our experiment. One door and the window frame had been plastered round with varnished paper so as to be practically sealed. Above the other door, which opened on to the landing, there hung a fanlight which could be drawn by a cord when some ventilation became absolutely necessary. A large shrub in a tub stood in each corner.

'How to get rid of our excessive carbon dioxide without unduly wasting our oxygen is a delicate and vital question,' said Challenger, looking round him after the five iron tubes had been laid side by side against the wall. 'With longer time for preparation I could have brought the whole concentrated force of my intelligence to bear more fully upon the problem, but as it is we must do what we can. The shrubs will be of some small service. Two of the oxygen tubes are ready to be turned on at an instant's notice, so that we cannot be taken unawares. At the same time, it would be well not to go far from the room, as the crisis may be a sudden and urgent one.'

There was a broad, low window opening out upon a balcony. The view beyond was the same as that which we had already admired from the study. Looking out, I could see no sign of disorder anywhere. There was a road curving down the side of the hill, under my very eyes. A cab from the station, one of those prehistoric survivals which are only to be found in our country villages, was toiling slowly up the hill. Lower down was a nurse girl wheeling a perambulator and leading a second child by the hand. The blue reeks of smoke from the cottages gave the whole widespread landscape an air of settled order and homely comfort. Nowhere in the blue heaven or on the sunlit earth was there any foreshadowing of a catastrophe. The harvesters were back in the fields once more and the golfers, in pairs and fours, were still streaming round the links. There was so strange a turmoil within my own head, and such a jangling of my overstrung nerves, that the indifference of those people was amazing.

'Those fellows don't seem to feel any ill effects,' said I, pointing down at the links.

'Have you played golf?' asked Lord John.

'No, I have not.'

'Well, young fellah, when you do you'll learn that once fairly out on a round, it would take the crack of doom to stop a true golfer. Halloa! There's that telephone bell again.'

From time to time during and after lunch the high, insistent ring had summoned the Professor. He gave us the news as it came through to him in a few curt sentences. Such terrific items had never been registered in the world's history before. The great shadow was creeping up from the south like a rising tide of death. Egypt had gone through its delirium and was now comatose. Spain and Portugal, after a wild frenzy in which the Clericals and the Anarchists had fought most desperately, were now fallen silent. No cable messages were received any longer from South America. In North America the southern states, after some terrible racial rioting, had succumbed to the poison. North of Maryland the effect was not yet marked, and in Canada it was hardly perceptible. Belgium, Holland, and Denmark had each in turn been affected. Despairing messages were flashing from every quarter to the great centres of learning, to the chemists and the doctors of worldwide repute, imploring their advice. The astronomers too were deluged with inquiries. Nothing could be done. The thing was universal and beyond our human knowledge or control. It was death – painless but inevitable – death for young and old, for weak and strong, for rich and poor, without hope or possibility of escape. Such was the news which, in scattered, distracted messages, the telephone had brought us. The great cities already knew their fate, and so far as we could gather were preparing to meet it with dignity and resignation. Yet here were our golfers and labourers like the lambs who gambol under the shadow of the knife. It seemed amazing. And yet how could they know? It had all come upon us in one giant stride. What was there in the morning paper to alarm them? And now it was but three in the afternoon. Even as we looked some rumour seemed to have spread, for we saw the reapers hurrying from the fields. Some of the golfers were returning to the clubhouse. They were running as if taking refuge from a shower. Their little caddies trailed behind them. Others were continuing their game. The nurse had turned and was pushing her perambulator hurriedly up the hill again. I noticed that she had her hand to her brow. The cab had stopped and the tired horse, with his head sunk to his knees, was resting. Above there was a perfect summer sky – one huge vault of un-broken blue, save for a few fleecy white clouds over the distant downs. If the human race must die today, it was at least upon a glorious deathbed. And yet all that gentle loveliness of nature made this terrific and wholesale destruction the more pitiable and awful. Surely it was too goodly a residence that we should be so swiftly, so ruthlessly, evicted from it!

But I have said that the telephone bell had rung once more. Suddenly I heard Challenger's tremendous voice from the hall.

'Malone!' he cried. 'You are wanted.'

I rushed down to the instrument. It was McArdle speaking from London.

'That you, Mr Malone?' cried his familiar voice. 'Mr Malone, there are terrible goings-on in London. For God's sake, see if Professor Challenger can suggest anything that can be done.'

'He can suggest nothing, sir,' I answered. 'He regards the crisis as universal and inevitable. We have some oxygen here, but it can only defer our fate for a few hours.'

'Oxygen!' cried the agonised voice. 'There is no time to get any. The office has been a perfect pandemonium ever since you left in the morning. Now half of the staff are insensible. I am weighed down with heaviness myself. From my window I can see the people lying thick in Fleet Street. The traffic is all held up. Judging by the last telegrams, the whole world –'

His voice had been sinking, and suddenly stopped. An instant later I heard through the telephone a muffled thud, as if his head had fallen forward on the desk.

'Mr McArdle!' I cried. 'Mr McArdle!'

There was no answer. I knew as I replaced the receiver that I should never hear his voice again.

At that instant, just as I took a step backwards from the telephone, the thing was on us. It was as if we were bathers, up to our shoulders in water, who suddenly are submerged by a rolling wave. An invisible hand seemed to have quietly closed round my throat and to be gently pressing the life from me. I was conscious of immense oppression upon my chest, great tightness within my head, a loud singing in my ears, and bright flashes before my eyes. I staggered to the balustrades of the stair. At the same moment, rushing and snorting like a wounded buffalo, Challenger dashed past me, a terrible vision, with red-purple face, engorged eyes, and bristling hair. His little wife, insensible to all appearance, was slung over his great shoulder, and he blundered and thundered up the stair, scrambling and tripping, but carrying himself and her through sheer will-force through that mephitic atmosphere to the haven of temporary safety. At the sight of his effort I too rushed up the steps, clambering, falling, clutching at the rail, until I tumbled half senseless upon by face on the upper landing. Lord John's fingers of steel were in the collar of my coat, and a moment later I was stretched upon my back, unable to speak or move, on the boudoir carpet. The woman lay beside me, and Summerlee was bunched in a chair by the window, his head nearly touching his knees. As in a dream I saw Challenger, like a monstrous beetle, crawling slowly across the floor, and a moment later I heard the gentle hissing of the escaping oxygen. Challenger breathed two or three times with enormous gulps, his lungs roaring as he drew in the vital gas.

'It works!' he cried exultantly. 'My reasoning has been justified!' He was up on his feet again, alert and strong. With a tube in his hand he rushed over to his wife and held it to her face. In a few seconds she moaned, stirred, and sat up. He turned to me, and I felt the tide of life stealing warmly through my arteries. My reason told me that it was but a little respite, and yet, carelessly as we talk of its value, every hour of existence now seemed an inestimable thing. Never have I known such a thrill of sensuous joy as came with that freshet of life. The weight fell away from my lungs, the band loosened from my brow, a sweet feeling of peace and gentle, languid comfort stole over me. I lay watching Summerlee revive under the same remedy, and finally Lord John took his turn. He sprang to his feet and gave me a hand to rise, while Challenger picked up his wife and laid her on the settee.

'Oh, George, I am so sorry you brought me back,' she said, holding him by the hand. 'The door of death is indeed, as you said, hung with beautiful, shimmering curtains; for, once the choking feeling had passed, it was all unspeakably soothing and beautiful. Why have you dragged me back?'

'Because I wish that we make the passage together. We have been together so many years. It would be sad to fall apart at the supreme moment.'

For a moment in his tender voice I caught a glimpse of a new Challenger, something very far from the bullying, ranting, arrogant man who had alternately amazed and offended his generation. Here in the shadow of death was the innermost Challenger, the man who had won and held a woman's love. Suddenly his mood changed and he was our strong captain once again.

'Alone of all mankind I saw and foretold this catastrophe,' said he with a ring of exultation and scientific triumph in his voice. 'As to you, my good Summerlee, I trust your last doubts have been resolved as to the meaning of the blurring of the lines in the spectrum and that you will no longer contend that my letter in *The Times* was based upon a delusion.'

For once our pugnacious colleague was deaf to a challenge. He could but sit gasping and stretching his long, thin limbs, as if to assure himself that he was still really upon this planet. Challenger walked across to the oxygen tube, and the sound of the loud hissing fell away till it was the most gentle sibilation.

'We must husband our supply of the gas,' said he. 'The atmosphere of the room is now strongly hyperoxygenated, and I take it that none of us feel any distressing symptoms. We can only determine by actual experiments what amount added to the air will serve to neutralise the poison. Let us see how that will do.'

We sat in silent nervous tension for five minutes or more, observing our own sensations. I had just begun to fancy that I felt the constriction round my temples again when Mrs Challenger called out from the sofa that she was fainting. Her husband turned on more gas.

'In pre-scientific days,' said he, 'they used to keep a white mouse in every submarine, as its more delicate organisation

44

gave signs of a vicious atmosphere before it was perceived by the sailors. You, my dear, will be our white mouse. I have now increased the supply and you are better.'

'Yes, I am better.'

'Possibly we have hit upon the correct mixture. When we have ascertained exactly how little will serve we shall be able to compute how long we shall be able to exist. Unfortunately, in resuscitating ourselves we have already consumed a considerable proportion of this first tube.'

'Does it matter?' asked Lord John, who was standing with his hands in his pockets close to the window. 'If we have to go, what is the use of holdin' on? You don't suppose there's any chance for us?'

Challenger smiled and shook his head.

'Well, then, don't you think there is more dignity in takin' the jump and not waitin' to be pushed in? If it must be so, I'm for sayin' our prayers, turnin' off the gas, and openin' the window.'

'Why not?' said the lady bravely. 'Surely, George, Lord John is right and it is better so.'

'I most strongly object,' cried Summerlee in a querulous voice. 'When we must die let us by all means die, but to deliberately anticipate death seems to me to be a foolish and unjustifiable action.'

'What does our young friend say to it?' asked Challenger.

'I think we should see it to the end.'

'And I am strongly of the same opinion,' said he.

'Then, George, if you say so, I think so too,' cried the lady.

'Well, well, I'm only puttin' it as an argument,' said Lord John. 'If you all want to see it through I am with you. It's dooced interestin', and no mistake about that. I've had my share of adventures in my life, and as many thrills as most folk, but I'm endin' on my top note.'

'Granting the continuity of life,' said Challenger.

'A large assumption!' cried Summerlee. Challenger stared at him in silent reproof.

'Granting the continuity of life,' said he, in his most didactic manner, 'none of us can predicate what opportunities of observation one may have from what we may call the spirit plane to the plane of matter. It surely must be evident to the most obtuse person' (here he glared at Summerlee) 'that it is while we are ourselves material that we are most fitted to watch and form a judgment upon material phenomena. Therefore it is only by keeping alive for these few extra hours that we can hope to carry on with us to some future existence a clear conception of the most stupendous event that the world, or the universe so far as we know it, has ever encountered. To me it would seem a deplorable thing that we should in any way curtail by so much as a minute so wonderful an experience.'

'I am strongly of the same opinion,' cried Summerlee.

'Carried without a division,' said Lord John. 'By George, that poor devil of a chauffeur of yours down in the yard has made his last journey. No use makin' a sally and bringin' him in?'

'It would be absolute madness,' cried Summerlee.

'Well, I suppose it would,' said Lord John. 'It couldn't help him and would scatter our gas all over the house, even if we ever got back alive. My word, look at the little birds under the trees!'

We drew four chairs up to the long, low window, the lady still resting with closed eyes upon the settee. I remember that the monstrous and grotesque idea crossed my mind – the illusion may have been heightened by the heavy stuffiness of the air which we were breathing – that we were in four front seats of the stalls at the last act of the drama of the world.

In the immediate foreground, beneath our very eyes, was the small yard with the half-cleaned motor car standing in it. Austin, the chauffeur, had received his final notice at last, for he was sprawling beside the wheel, with a great black bruise upon his forehead where it had struck the step or mudguard in falling. He still held in his hand the nozzle of the hose with which he had been washing down his machine. A couple of small plane trees stood in the corner of the yard, and underneath them lay several pathetic little balls of fluffy feathers, with tiny feet uplifted. The sweep of death's scythe had included everything, great and small, within its swathe.

Over the wall of the yard we looked down upon the winding road, which led to the station. A group of the reapers whom we had seen running from the fields were lying all pell-mell, their bodies crossing each other, at the bottom of it. Farther up, the nurse girl lay with her head and shoulders propped against the slope of the grassy bank. She had taken the baby from the perambulator, and it was a motionless bundle of wraps in her arms. Close behind her a tiny patch upon the roadside showed where the little boy was stretched. Still nearer to us was the dead cab-horse, kneeling between the shafts. The old driver was hanging over the splashboard like some grotesque scarecrow, his arms dangling absurdly in front of him. Through the window we could dimly discern that a young man was seated inside. The door was swinging open and his hand was grasping the handle, as if he had attempted to leap forth at the last instant. In the middle distance lay the golf links, dotted as they had been in the morning with the dark figures of the golfers, lying motionless upon the grass of the course or among the heather which skirted it. On one particular green there were eight bodies stretched where a foursome with its caddies had held to their game to the last. No bird flew in the blue vault of heaven, no man or beast moved upon the vast countryside which lay before us. The evening sun shone its peaceful radiance across it, but there brooded over it all the stillness and the silence of universal death – a death in which we were so soon to join. At the present instant that one frail sheet of glass, by holding in the extra oxygen which counteracted the poisoned ether, shut us off from the fate of all our kind. For a few short hours the knowledge and foresight of one man could preserve our little oasis of life in the vast desert of death and save us from participation in the common catastrophe. Then the gas would run low, we too should lie gasping upon that cherry-coloured boudoir carpet, and the fate of the human race and of all earthly life would be complete. For a long time, in a mood which was too solemn for speech, we looked out at the tragic world.

'There is a house on fire,' said Challenger at last, pointing to a column of smoke which rose above the trees. 'There will, I expect, be many such – possibly whole cities in flames – when we consider how many folk may have dropped with lights in their hands. The fact of combustion is in itself enough to show that the proportion of oxygen in the atmosphere is normal, and that it is the ether which is at fault. Ah, there you see another blaze on the top of Crowborough Hill. It is the golf clubhouse, or I am mistaken. There is the church clock chiming the hour. It would interest our philosophers to know that manmade mechanism has survived the race who made it.'

'By George!' cried Lord John, rising excitedly from his chair. 'What's that puff of smoke? It's a train.'

We heard the roar of it, and presently it came flying into sight, going at what seemed to me to be a prodigious speed. Whence it had come, or how far, we had no means of knowing. Only by some miracle of luck could it have gone any distance. But now we were to see the terrific end of its career. A train of coal trucks stood motionless upon the line. We held our breath as the express roared along the same track. The crash was horrible. Engine and carriages piled themselves into a hill of splintered wood and twisted iron. Red spurts of flame flickered up from the wreckage until it was all ablaze. For half an hour we sat with hardly a word, stunned by the stupendous sight.

'Poor, poor people!' cried Mrs. Challenger at last, clinging with a whimper to her husband's arm.

'My dear, the passengers on that train were no more animate than the coals into which they crashed or the carbon which they have now become,' said Challenger, stroking her hand soothingly. 'It was a train of the living when it left Victoria, but it was driven and freighted by the dead long before it reached its fate.'

'All over the world the same thing must be going on,' said I as a vision of strange happenings rose before me. 'Think of the ships at sea – how they will steam on and on, until the furnaces die down or until they run full tilt upon some beach. The sailing ships, too – how they will back and fill with their cargoes of dead sailors, while their timbers rot and their joints leak, till one by one they sink below the surface. Perhaps a century hence the Atlantic may still be dotted with the old drifting derelicts.'

'And the folk in the coal mines,' said Summerlee with a dismal chuckle. 'If ever geologists should by any chance live upon earth again they will have some strange theories of the existence of man in carboniferous strata.'

'I don't profess to know about such things,' remarked Lord John, 'but it seems to me the earth will be "To let, empty", after this. When once our human crowd is wiped off it, how will it ever get on again?'

'The world was empty before,' Challenger answered gravely. 'Under laws which in their inception are beyond and above us, it became peopled. Why may the same process not happen again?'

'My dear Challenger, you can't mean that?'

'I am not in the habit, Professor Summerlee, of saying things which I do not mean. The observation is trivial.' Out went the beard and down came the eyelids.

'Well, you lived an obstinate dogmatist, and you mean to die one,' said Summerlee sourly.

'And you, sir, have lived an unimaginative obstructionist and never can hope now to emerge from it.'

'Your worst critics will never accuse you of lacking imagination,' Summerlee retorted.

'Upon my word!' said Lord John. 'It would be like you if you used up our last gasp of oxygen in abusin' each other. What can it matter whether folk come back or not? It surely won't be in our time.'

'In that remark, sir, you betray your own very pronounced limitations,' said Challenger severely. 'The true scientific mind is not to be tied down by its own conditions of time and space. It builds itself an observatory erected upon the border line of the present, which separates the infinite past from the infinite future. From this sure post it makes its sallies even to the beginning and to the end of all things. As to death, the scientific mind dies at its post working in normal and methodic fashion to the end. It disregards so petty a thing as its own physical dissolution as completely as it does all other limitations upon the plane of matter. Am I right, Professor Summerlee?'

Summerlee grumbled an ungracious assent.

'With certain reservations, I agree,' said he.

'The ideal scientific mind,' continued Challenger, 'I put it in the third person rather than appear to be too self-complacent – the ideal scientific mind should be capable of thinking out a point of abstract knowledge in the interval between its owner falling from a balloon and reaching the earth. Men of this strong fibre are needed to form the conquerors of nature and the body-guard of truth.'

'It strikes me nature's on top this time,' said Lord John, looking out of the window. 'I've read some leadin' articles about you gentlemen controllin' her, but she's gettin' a bit of her own back.'

'It is but a temporary setback,' said Challenger with conviction. 'A few million years, what are they in the great cycle of time? The vegetable world has, as you can see, survived. Look at the leaves of that plane tree. The birds are dead, but the plant flourishes. From this vegetable life in pond and in marsh will come, in time, the tiny crawling microscopic slugs which are the pioneers of that great army of life in which for the instant we five have the extraordinary duty of serving as rearguard. Once the lowest form of life has established itself, the final advent of man is as certain as the growth of the oak from the acorn. The old circle will swing round once more.'

'But the poison?' I asked. 'Will that not nip life in the bud?'

'The poison may be a mere stratum or layer in the ether – a mephitic Gulf Stream across that mighty ocean in which we float. Or tolerance may be established, and life accommodate itself to a new condition. The mere fact that with a comparatively small hyperoxygenation of our blood we can hold out against it is surely a proof in itself that no very great change would be needed to enable animal life to endure it.'

The smoking house beyond the trees had burst into flames. We could see the high tongues of fire shooting up into the air.

'It's pretty awful,' muttered Lord John, more impressed than I had ever seen him.

'Well, after all, what does it matter?' I remarked. 'The world is dead. Cremation is surely the best burial.'

'It would shorten us up if this house went ablaze.'

'I foresaw the danger,' said Challenger, 'and asked my wife to guard against it.'

'Everything is quite safe, dear. But my head begins to throb again. What a dreadful atmosphere!'

'We must change it,' said Challenger. He bent over his cylinder of oxygen.

'It's nearly empty,' said he. 'It has lasted us some three and a half hours. It is now close on eight o'clock. We shall get through the night comfortably. I should expect the end about nine o'clock tomorrow morning. We shall see one sunrise, which shall be all our own.'

He turned on his second tube and opened for half a minute the fanlight over the door. Then as the air became perceptibly better, but our own symptoms more acute, he closed it once again.

'By the way,' said he, 'man does not live upon oxygen alone. It's dinnertime and over. I assure you, gentlemen, that when I invited you to my home and to what I had hoped would be an interesting reunion, I had intended that my kitchen should justify itself. However, we must do what we can. I am sure that you will agree with me that it would be folly to consume our air too rapidly by lighting an oil-stove. I have some small provision of cold meats, bread, and pickles, which, with a couple of bottles of claret, may serve our turn. Thank you, my dear – now as ever you are the queen of managers.'

It was indeed wonderful how, with the self-respect and sense of propriety of the British housekeeper, the lady had within a few minutes adorned the central table with a snow-white cloth, laid the napkins upon it, and set forth the simple meal with all the elegance of civilisation, including an electric torch lamp in the centre. Wonderful also was it to find that our appetites were ravenous.

'It is the measure of our emotion,' said Challenger with that air of condescension with which he brought his scientific mind to the explanation of humble facts. 'We have gone through a great crisis. That means molecular disturbance. That in turn means the need for repair. Great sorrow or great joy should bring intense hunger – not abstinence from food, as our novelists will have it.'

'That's why the country folk have great feasts at funerals,' I hazarded.

'Exactly. Our young friend has hit upon an excellent illustration. Let me give you another slice of tongue.'

'The same with savages,' said Lord John, cutting away at the beef. 'I've seen them buryin' a chief up the Aruwimi River, and they ate a hippo that must have weighed as much as a tribe. There are some of them down New Guinea way that eat the late-lamented himself, just by way of a last tidy up. Well, of all the funeral feasts on this earth, I suppose the one we are takin' is the queerest.'

'The strange thing is,' said Mrs Challenger, 'that I find it impossible to feel grief for those who are gone. There are my father and mother at Bedford. I know that they are dead, and yet in this tremendous universal tragedy I can feel no sharp sorrow for any individuals, even for them.'

'And my old mother in her cottage in Ireland,' said I. 'I can see her in my mind's eye, with her shawl and her lace cap, lying back with closed eyes in the old high-backed chair near the window, her glasses and her book beside her. Why should I mourn her? She has passed and I am passing, and I may be nearer her in some other life than England is to Ireland. Yet I grieve to think that that dear body is no more.'

'As to the body,' remarked Challenger, 'we do not mourn over the parings of our nails nor the cut locks of our hair, though they were once part of ourselves. Neither does a one-legged man yearn sentimentally over his missing member. The physical body has rather been a source of pain and fatigue to us. It is the constant index of our limitations. Why then should we worry about its detachment from our psychical selves?'

'If they can indeed be detached,' Summerlee grumbled. 'But, anyhow, universal death is dreadful.'

'As I have already explained,' said Challenger, 'a universal death must in its nature be far less terrible than an isolated one.'

'Same in a battle,' remarked Lord John. 'If you saw a single man lying on that floor with his chest knocked in and a hole in his face it would turn you sick. But I've seen ten thousand on their backs in the Sudan, and it gave me no such feelin', for when you are makin' history the life of any man is too small a thing to worry over. When a thousand million pass over together, same as happened today, you can't pick your own partic'lar out of the crowd.'

'I wish it were well over with us,' said the lady wistfully. 'Oh, George, I am so frightened.'

'You'll be the bravest of us all, little lady, when the time comes. I've been a blusterous old husband to you, dear, but you'll just bear in mind that G.E.C. is as he was made and couldn't help himself. After all, you wouldn't have had anyone else?'

'No one in the whole wide world, dear,' said she, and put her arms round his bull neck. We three walked to the window and stood amazed at the sight which met our eyes.

Darkness had fallen and the dead world was shrouded in gloom. But right across the southern horizon was one long vivid scarlet streak, waxing and waning in vivid pulses of life, leaping suddenly to a crimson zenith and then dying down to a glowing line of fire.

'Lewes is ablaze!'

'No, it is Brighton which is burning,' said Challenger, stepping across to join us. 'You can see the curved back of the downs against the glow. That fire is miles on the farther side of it. The whole town must be alight.'

There were several red glares at different points, and the pile of debris upon the railway line was still smouldering darkly, but they all seemed mere pinpoints of light compared to that monstrous conflagration throbbing beyond the hills. What copy it would have made for the *Gazette*! Had ever a journalist such an opening and so little chance of using it – the scoop of scoops, and no one to appreciate it? And then, suddenly, the old instinct of recording came over me. If these men of science could be so true to their life's work to the very end, why should not I, in my humble way, be as constant? No human eye might ever rest upon what I had done. But the long night had to be passed somehow, and for me at least, sleep seemed to be out of the question. My notes would help to pass the weary hours and to occupy my thoughts. Thus it is that now I have before me the notebook with its scribbled pages, written confusedly upon my knee in the dim, waning light of our one electric torch. Had I the literary touch, they might have been worthy of the occasion. As it is, they may still serve to bring to other minds the long-drawn emotions and tremors of that awful night.

4

A Diary of the Dying

How strange the words look scribbled at the top of the empty page of my book! How stranger still that it is I, Edward Malone, who have written them – I who started only some twelve hours ago from my rooms in Streatham without one thought of the marvels which the day was to bring forth! I look back at the chain of incidents, my interview with McArdle, Challenger's first note of alarm in *The Times*, the absurd journey in the train, the pleasant luncheon, the catastrophe, and now it has come to this – that we linger alone upon an empty planet, and so sure is our fate that I can regard these lines, written from mechanical professional habit and never to be seen by human eyes, as the words of one who is already dead, so closely does he stand to the shadowed borderland over which all outside this one little circle of friends have already gone. I feel how wise and true were the words of Challenger when he said that the real tragedy would be if we were left behind when all that is noble and good and beautiful had passed. But of that there can surely be no danger. Already our second tube of oxygen is drawing to an end. We can count the poor dregs of our lives almost to a minute.

We have just been treated to a lecture, a good quarter of an hour long, from Challenger, who was so excited that he roared and bellowed as if he were addressing his old rows of scientific sceptics in the Queen's Hall. He had certainly a strange audience to harangue: his wife perfectly acquiescent and absolutely ignorant of his meaning, Summerlee seated in the shadow, querulous and critical but interested, Lord John lounging in a corner somewhat bored by the whole proceeding, and myself beside the window watching the scene with a kind of detached attention, as if it were all a dream or something in which I had no personal interest whatever. Challenger sat at the centre table with the electric light illuminating the slide under the microscope which he had brought from his dressing room. The small vivid circle of white light from the mirror left half of his rugged, bearded face in brilliant radiance and half in deepest shadow. He had, it seems, been working of late upon the lowest forms of life, and what excited him at the present moment was that in the microscopic slide made up the day before he found the amoeba to be still alive.

'You can see it for yourselves,' he kept repeating in great excitement. 'Summerlee, will you step across and satisfy yourself upon the point? Malone, will you kindly verify what I say? The little spindle-shaped things in the centre are diatoms and may be disregarded since they are probably vegetable rather than animal. But the right-hand side you will see an undoubted amoeba, moving sluggishly across the field. The upper screw is the fine adjustment. Look at it for yourselves.'

Summerlee did so, and acquiesced. So did I and perceived a little creature which looked as if it were made of ground glass flowing in a sticky way across the lighted circle. Lord John was prepared to take him on trust.

'I'm not troublin' my head whether he's alive or dead,' said he. 'We don't so much as know each other by sight, so why should I take it to heart? I don't suppose he's worryin' himself over the state of *our* health.'

I laughed at this, and Challenger looked in my direction with his coldest and most supercilious stare. It was a most petrifying experience.

'The flippancy of the half-educated is more obstructive to science than the obtuseness of the ignorant,' said he. 'If Lord John Roxton would condescend –'

'My dear George, don't be so peppery,' said his wife, with her hand on the black mane that drooped over the microscope. 'What can it matter whether the amoeba is alive or not?'

'It matters a great deal,' said Challenger gruffly.

'Well, let's hear about it,' said Lord John with a good-humoured smile. 'We may as well talk about that as anything else. If you think I've been too offhand with the thing, or hurt its feelin's in any way, I'll apologise.'

'For my part,' remarked Summerlee in his creaky, argumentative voice, 'I can't see why you should attach such importance to the creature being alive. It is in the same atmosphere as ourselves, so naturally the poison does not act upon it. If it were outside of this room it would be dead, like all other animal life.'

'Your remarks, my good Summerlee,' said Challenger with enormous condescension (oh, if I could paint that overbearing, arrogant face in the vivid circle of reflection from the microscope mirror!) 'your remarks show that you imperfectly appreciate the situation. This specimen was mounted yesterday and is hermetically sealed. None of our oxygen can reach it. But the ether, of course, has penetrated to it, as to every other point upon the universe. Therefore, it has survived the poison. Hence, we may argue that every amoeba outside this room, instead of being dead, as you have erroneously stated, has really survived the catastrophe.'

'Well, even now I don't feel inclined to hip-hurrah about it,' said Lord John. 'What does it matter?'

'It just matters this, that the world is a living instead of a dead one. If you had the scientific imagination, you would cast your mind forward from this one fact, and you would see some few millions of years hence – a mere passing moment in the enormous flux of the ages – the whole world teeming once more with the animal and human life which will spring from this tiny root. You have seen a prairie fire, where the flames have swept every trace of grass or plant from the surface of the earth and left only a blackened waste. Yet the roots of growth have been left behind, and when you pass the place a few years hence you can no longer tell where the black scars used to be. Here in this tiny creature are the roots of growth of the animal world, and by its inherent development, and evolution, it will surely in time remove every trace of this incomparable crisis in which we are now involved.'

'Dooced interestin'!' said Lord John, lounging across and looking through the microscope. 'Funny little chap to hang number one among the family portraits. Got a fine big shirt-stud on him!'

'The dark object is his nucleus,' said Challenger with the air of a nurse teaching letters to a baby.

'Well, we needn't feel lonely,' said Lord John laughing. 'There's somebody livin' besides us on the earth.'

'You seem to take it for granted, Challenger,' said Summerlee, 'that the object for which this world was created was that it should produce and sustain human life.'

'Well, sir, and what object do you suggest?' asked Challenger, bristling at the least hint of contradiction.

'Sometimes I think that it is only the monstrous conceit of mankind which makes him think that all this stage was erected for him to strut upon.'

'We cannot be dogmatic about it, but at least without what you have ventured to call monstrous conceit we can surely say that we are the highest thing in nature.'

'The highest of which we have cognisance.'

'That, sir, goes without saying.'

'Think of all the millions and possibly billions of years that the earth swung empty through space – or, if not empty, at least without a sign or thought of the human race. Think of it, washed by the rain and scorched by the sun and swept by the wind for those unnumbered ages. Man only came into being yesterday so far as geological times goes. Why, then, should it be taken for granted that all this stupendous preparation was for his benefit?'

'For whose then – or for what?'

Summerlee shrugged his shoulders.

'How can we tell? For some reason altogether beyond our conception – and man may have been a mere accident, a by-product evolved in the process. It is as if the scum upon the surface of the ocean imagined that the ocean was created in order to produce and sustain it, or a mouse in a cathedral thought that the building was its own proper ordained residence.'

I have jotted down the very words of their argument, but now it degenerates into a mere noisy wrangle with much polysyllabic scientific jargon upon each side. It is no doubt a privilege to hear two such brains discuss the highest questions; but as they are in perpetual disagreement, plain folk like Lord John and I get little that is positive from the exhibition. They neutralise each other and we are left as they found us. Now the hubbub has ceased, and Summerlee is coiled up in his chair, while Challenger, still fingering the screws of his microscope, is keeping up a continual low, deep, inarticulate growl like the sea after a storm. Lord John comes over to me, and we look out together into the night.

There is a pale new moon – the last moon that human eyes will ever rest upon – and the stars are most brilliant. Even in the clear plateau air of South America I have never seen them brighter. Possibly this etheric change has some effect upon light. The funeral pyre of Brighton is still blazing, and there is a very distant patch of scarlet in the western sky, which may mean trouble at Arundel or Chichester, possibly even at Portsmouth. I sit and muse and make an occasional note. There is a sweet melancholy in the air. Youth and beauty and chivalry and love – is this to be the end of it all? The starlit earth looks a dreamland of gentle peace. Who would imagine it as the terrible Golgotha strewn with the bodies of the human race? Suddenly, I find myself laughing.

'Halloa, young fellah!' says Lord John, staring at me in surprise. 'We could do with a joke in these hard times. What was it, then?'

'I was thinking of all the great unsolved questions,' I answer, 'the questions that we spent so much labour and thought over. Think of Anglo-German competition, for example – or the Persian Gulf that my old chief was so keen about. Whoever would have guessed, when we fumed and fretted so, how they were to be eventually solved?'

We fall into silence again. I fancy that each of us is thinking of friends that have gone before. Mrs Challenger is sobbing quietly, and her husband is whispering to her. My mind turns to all the most unlikely people, and I see each of them lying white and rigid as poor Austin does in the yard. There is McArdle, for example, I know exactly where he is, with his face upon his writing desk and his hand on his own telephone, just as I heard him fall. Beaumont, the editor, too – I suppose he is lying upon the blue and red Turkey carpet which adorned his sanctum. And the fellows in the reporters' room – Macdonna and Murray and Bond. They had certainly died hard at work on their job, with notebooks full of vivid impressions and strange happenings in their hands. I could just imagine how this one would have been packed off to the doctors, and that other to Westminster, and yet a third to St Paul's. What glorious rows of headlines they must have seen as a last vision beautiful, never destined to materialise in printer's ink! I could see Macdonna among the doctors – 'Hope in Harley Street' – Mac had always a weakness for alliteration. 'Interview with Mr Soley Wilson.' 'Famous Specialist says "Never despair!"' 'Our Special Correspondent found the eminent scientist seated upon the roof, whither he had retreated to avoid the crowd of terrified patients who had stormed his dwelling. With a manner which plainly showed his appreciation of the immense gravity of the occasion, the celebrated physician refused to admit that every avenue of hope had been closed.' That's how Mac would start. Then there was Bond; he would probably do St Paul's. He fancied his own literary touch. My word, what a theme for him! 'Standing in the little gallery under the dome and looking down upon that packed mass of despairing humanity, grovelling at this last instant before a Power which they had so persistently ignored, there rose to my ears from the swaying crowd such a low moan of entreaty and terror, such a shuddering cry for help to the Unknown, that –' and so forth.

Yes, it would be a great end for a reporter, though, like myself, he would die with the treasures still unused. What would Bond not give, poor chap, to see 'J.H.B.' at the foot of a column like that?

But what drivel I am writing! It is just an attempt to pass the weary time. Mrs Challenger has gone to the inner dressing room, and the Professor says that she is asleep. He is making notes and consulting books at the central table, as calmly as if years of placid work lay before him. He writes with a very noisy quill pen which seems to be screeching scorn at all who disagree with him.

Summerlee has dropped off in his chair and gives from time to time a peculiarly exasperating snore. Lord John lies back with his hands in his pockets and his eyes closed. How people can sleep under such conditions is more than I can imagine.

Three thirty a.m. I have just wakened with a start. It was five minutes past eleven when I made my last entry. I remember winding up my watch and noting the time. So I have wasted some five hours of the little span still left to us. Who would have believed it possible? But I feel very much fresher, and ready for my fate – or try to persuade myself that I am. And yet, the fitter a man is, and the higher his tide of life, the more must he shrink from death. How wise and how merciful is that provision of nature by which his earthly anchor is usually loosened by many little imperceptible tugs, until his consciousness has drifted out of its untenable earthly harbour into the great sea beyond!

Mrs Challenger is still in the dressing room. Challenger has fallen asleep in his chair. What a picture! His enormous frame leans back, his huge, hairy hands are clasped across his waistcoat, and his head is so tilted that I can see nothing above his collar save a tangled bristle of luxuriant beard. He shakes with the vibration of his own snoring. Summerlee adds his occasional high tenor to Challenger's sonorous bass. Lord John is sleeping also, his long body doubled up sideways in a basket-chair. The first cold light of dawn is just stealing into the room, and everything is grey and mournful.

I look out at the sunrise – that fateful sunrise which will shine upon an unpeopled world. The human race is gone, extinguished in a day, but the planets swing round and the tides rise or fall, and the wind whispers, and all nature goes her way, down, as it would seem, to the very amoeba, with never a sign that he who styled himself the lord of creation had ever blessed or cursed the universe with his presence. Down in the yard lies Austin with sprawling limbs, his face glimmering white in the dawn, and the hose nozzle still projecting from his dead hand. The whole of human kind is typified in that one half-ludicrous and half-pathetic figure, lying so helpless beside the machine which it used to control.

Here end the notes which I made at the time. Henceforward events were too swift and too poignant to allow me to write, but they are too clearly outlined in my memory that any detail could escape me.

Some chokiness in my throat made me look at the oxygen cylinders, and I was startled at what I saw. The sands of our lives were running very low. At some period in the night Challenger had switched the tube from the third to the fourth cylinder. Now it was clear that this also was nearly exhausted. That horrible feeling of constriction was closing in upon me. I ran across and, unscrewing the nozzle, I changed it to our last supply. Even as I did so my conscience pricked me, for I felt that perhaps if I had held my hand all of them might have passed in their sleep. The thought was banished, however, by the voice of the lady from the inner room crying:–

'George, George, I am stifling!'

'It is all right, Mrs Challenger,' I answered as the others started to their feet. 'I have just turned on a fresh supply.'

Even at such a moment I could not help smiling at Challenger, who with a great hairy fist in each eye was like a huge, bearded baby, new wakened out of sleep. Summerlee was shivering like a man with the ague, human fears, as he realised his position, rising for an instant above the stoicism of the man of science. Lord John, however, was as cool and alert as if he had just been roused on a hunting morning.

'Fifthly and lastly,' said he, glancing at the tube. 'Say, young fellah, don't tell me you've been writin' up your impressions in that paper on your knee.'

'Just a few notes to pass the time.'

'Well, I don't believe anyone but an Irishman would have done that. I expect you'll have to wait till little brother amoeba gets grown up before you'll find a reader. He don't seem to take much stock of things at just present. Well, Herr Professor, what are the prospects?'

Challenger was looking out at the great drifts of morning mist which lay over the landscape. Here and there the wooded hills rose like conical islands out of this woolly sea.

'It might be a winding sheet,' said Mrs Challenger, who had entered in her dressing gown. 'There's that song of yours, George, "Ring out the old, ring in the new". It was prophetic. But you are shivering, my poor dear friends. I have been warm under a coverlet all night, and you cold in your chairs. But I'll soon set you right.'

The brave little creature hurried away, and presently we heard the sizzling of a kettle. She was back soon with five steaming cups of cocoa upon a tray.

'Drink these,' said she. 'You will feel so much better.'

And we did. Summerlee asked if he might light his pipe, and we all had cigarettes. It steadied our nerves, I think, but it was a mistake, for it made a dreadful atmosphere in that stuffy room. Challenger had to open the ventilator.

'How long, Challenger?' asked Lord John.

'Possibly three hours,' he answered with a shrug.

'I used to be frightened,' said his wife. 'But the nearer I get to it, the easier it seems. Don't you think we ought to pray, George?'

'You will pray, dear, if you wish,' the big man answered, very gently. 'We all have our own ways of praying. Mine is a complete acquiescence in whatever fate may send me – a cheerful acquiescence. The highest religion and the highest science seem to unite on that.'

'I cannot truthfully describe my mental attitude as acquiescence and far less cheerful acquiescence,' grumbled Summerlee over his pipe. 'I submit because I have to. I confess that I should have liked another year of life to finish my classification of the chalk fossils.'

'Your unfinished work is a small thing,' said Challenger pompously, 'when weighed against the fact that my own *magnum opus*, "The Ladder of Life", is still in the first stages. My brain, my reading, my experience – in fact, my whole unique equipment – were to be condensed into that epoch-making volume. And yet, as I say, I acquiesce.'

'I expect we've all left some loose ends stickin' out,' said Lord John. 'What are yours, young fellah?'

'I was working at a book of verses,' I answered.

'Well, the world has escaped that, anyhow,' said Lord John. 'There's always compensation somewhere if you grope around.'

'What about you?' I asked.

'Well, it just so happens that I was tidied up and ready. I'd promised Merivale to go to Tibet for a snow leopard in the spring. But it's hard on you, Mrs Challenger, when you have just built up this pretty home.'

'Where George is, there is my home. But, oh, what would I not give for one last walk together in the fresh morning air upon those beautiful downs!'

Our hearts re-echoed her words. The sun had burst through the gauzy mists which veiled it, and the whole broad Weald was washed in golden light. Sitting in our dark and poisonous atmosphere that glorious, clean, windswept countryside seemed a very dream of beauty. Mrs Challenger held her hand stretched out to it in her longing. We drew up chairs and sat in a semicircle in the window. The atmosphere was already very close. It seemed to me that the shadows of death were drawing in upon us – the last of our race. It was like an invisible curtain closing down upon every side.

'That cylinder is not lastin' too well,' said Lord John with a long gasp for breath.

'The amount contained is variable,' said Challenger, 'depending upon the pressure and care with which it has been bottled. I am inclined to agree with you, Roxton, that this one is defective.'

'So we are to be cheated out of the last hour of our lives,' Summerlee remarked bitterly. 'An excellent final illustration of the sordid age in which we have lived. Well, Challenger, now is your time if you wish to study the subjective phenomena of physical dissolution.'

'Sit on the stool at my knee and give me your hand,' said Challenger to his wife. 'I think, my friends, that a further delay in this insufferable atmosphere is hardly advisable. You would not desire it, dear, would you?'

His wife gave a little groan and sank her face against his leg.

'I've seen the folk bathin' in the Serpentine in winter,' said Lord John. 'When the rest are in, you see one or two shiverin' on the bank, envyin' the others that have taken the plunge. It's the last that have the worst of it. I'm all for a header and have done with it.'

'You would open the window and face the ether?'

'Better be poisoned than stifled.'

Summerlee nodded his reluctant acquiescence and held out his thin hand to Challenger.

'We've had our quarrels in our time, but that's all over,' said he. 'We were good friends and had a respect for each other under the surface. Goodbye!'

'Goodbye, young fellah!' said Lord John. 'The window's plastered up. You can't open it.'

Challenger stooped and raised his wife, pressing her to his breast, while she threw her arms round his neck.

'Give me that field-glass, Malone,' said he gravely.

I handed it to him.

'Into the hands of the Power that made us we render ourselves again!' he shouted in his voice of thunder, and at the words he hurled the field glass through the window.

Full in our flushed faces, before the last tinkle of falling fragments had died away, there came the wholesome breath of the wind, blowing strong and sweet.

I don't know how long we sat in amazed silence. Then as in a dream, I heard Challenger's voice once more.

'We are back in normal conditions,' he cried. 'The world has cleared the poison belt, but we alone of all mankind are saved.'

5

The Dead World

I remember that we all sat gasping in our chairs, with that sweet, wet south-western breeze, fresh from the sea, flapping the muslin curtains and cooling our flushed faces. I wonder how long we sat! None of us afterwards could agree at all on that point. We were bewildered, stunned, semiconscious. We had all braced our courage for death, but this fearful and sudden new fact – that we must continue to live after we had survived the race to which we belonged – struck us with the shock of a physical blow and left us prostrate. Then gradually the suspended mechanism began to move once more; the shuttles of memory worked; ideas weaved themselves together in our minds. We saw, with vivid, merciless clearness, the relations between the past, the present, and the future – the lives that we had led and the lives which we would have to live. Our eyes turned in silent horror upon those of our companions and found the same answering look in theirs. Instead of the joy which men might have been expected to feel who had so narrowly escaped an imminent death, a terrible wave of darkest depression submerged us. Everything on earth that we loved had been washed away into the great, infinite, unknown ocean, and here were we marooned upon this desert island of a world, without companions, hopes, or aspirations. A few years' skulking like jackals among the graves of the human race and then our belated and lonely end would come.

'It's dreadful, George, dreadful!' the lady cried in an agony of sobs. 'If we had only passed with the others! Oh, why did you save us? I feel as if it is we that are dead and everyone else alive.'

Challenger's great eyebrows were drawn down in concentrated thought, while his huge, hairy paw closed upon the outstretched hand of his wife. I had observed that she always held out her arms to him in trouble as a child would to its mother.

'Without being a fatalist to the point of nonresistance,' said he, 'I have always found that the highest wisdom lies in an acquiescence with the actual.' He spoke slowly, and there was a vibration of feeling in his sonorous voice.

'I do *not* acquiesce,' said Summerlee firmly.

'I don't see that it matters a row of pins whether you acquiesce or whether you don't,' remarked Lord John. 'You've got to take it, whether you take it fightin' or take it lyin' down, so what's the odds whether you acquiesce or not?

'I can't remember that anyone asked our permission before the thing began, and nobody's likely to ask it now. So what difference can it make what we may think of it?'

'It is just all the difference between happiness and misery,' said Challenger with an abstracted face, still patting his wife's hand. 'You can swim with the tide and have peace in mind and soul, or you can thrust against it and be bruised and weary. This business is beyond us, so let us accept it as it stands and say no more.'

'But what in the world are we to do with our lives?' I asked, appealing in desperation to the blue, empty heaven.

'What am I to do, for example? There are no newspapers, so there's an end of my vocation.'

'And there's nothin' left to shoot, and no more soldierin', so there's an end of mine,' said Lord John.

'And there are no students, so there's an end of mine,' cried Summerlee.

'But I have my husband and my house, so I can thank heaven that there is no end of mine,' said the lady.

'Nor is there an end of mine,' remarked Challenger, 'for science is not dead, and this catastrophe in itself will offer us many most absorbing problems for investigation.'

He had now flung open the windows and we were gazing out upon the silent and motionless landscape.

'Let me consider,' he continued. 'It was about three, or a little after, yesterday afternoon that the world finally entered the poison belt to the extent of being completely submerged. It is now nine o'clock. The question is, at what hour did we pass out from it?'

'The air was very bad at daybreak,' said I.

'Later than that,' said Mrs Challenger. 'As late as eight o'clock I distinctly felt the same choking at my throat which came at the outset.'

'Then we shall say that it passed just after eight o'clock. For seventeen hours the world has been soaked in the poisonous ether. For that length of time the Great Gardener has sterilised the human mould which had grown over the surface of His fruit. Is it possible that the work is incompletely done – that others may have survived besides ourselves?'

'That's what I was wonderin'', said Lord John. 'Why should we be the only pebbles on the beach?'

'It is absurd to suppose that anyone besides ourselves can possibly have survived,' said Summerlee with conviction. 'Consider that the poison was so virulent that even a man who is as strong as an ox and has not a nerve in his body, like Malone here, could hardly get up the stairs before he fell unconscious. Is it likely that anyone could stand seventeen minutes of it, far less hours?'

'Unless someone saw it coming and made preparation, same as old friend Challenger did.'

'That, I think, is hardly probable,' said Challenger, projecting his beard and sinking his eyelids. 'The combination of observation, inference, and anticipatory imagination which enabled me to foresee the danger is what one can hardly expect twice in the same generation.'

'Then your conclusion is that everyone is certainly dead?'

'There can be little doubt of that. We have to remember, however, that the poison worked from below upwards and would possibly be less virulent in the higher strata of the atmosphere. It is strange, indeed, that it should be so; but it presents one of those features which will afford us in the future a fascinating field for study. One could imagine, therefore, that if one had to search for survivors one would turn one's eyes with best hopes of success to some Tibetan village or some Alpine farm, many thousands of feet above the sea level.'

'Well, considerin' that there are no railroads and no steamers you might as well talk about survivors in the moon,' said Lord John. 'But what I'm askin' myself is whether it's really over or whether it's only half-time.'

Summerlee craned his neck to look round the horizon. 'It seems clear and fine,' said he in a very dubious voice, 'but so it did yesterday. I am by no means assured that it is all over.'

Challenger shrugged his shoulders.

'We must come back once more to our fatalism,' said he. 'If the world has undergone this experience before, which is not outside the range of possibility, it was certainly a very long time ago. Therefore, we may reasonably hope that it will be very long before it occurs again.'

'That's all very well,' said Lord John, 'but if you get an earthquake shock you are mighty likely to have a second one right on the top of it. I think we'd be wise to stretch our legs and have a breath of air while we have the chance. Since our oxygen is exhausted we may just as well be caught outside as in.'

It was strange the absolute lethargy which had come upon us as a reaction after our tremendous emotions of the last twenty-four hours. It was both mental and physical, a deep-lying feeling that nothing mattered and that everything was a weariness and a profitless exertion. Even Challenger had succumbed to it, and sat in his chair, with his great head leaning upon his hands and his thoughts far away, until Lord John and I, catching him by each arm, fairly lifted him on to his feet, receiving only the glare and growl of an angry mastiff for our trouble. However, once we had got out of our narrow haven of refuge into the wider atmosphere of everyday life, our normal energy came gradually back to us once more.

But what were we to begin to do in that graveyard of a world? Could ever men have been faced with such a question since the dawn of time? It is true that our own physical needs, and even our luxuries, were assured for the future. All the stores of food, all the vintages of wine, all the treasures of art were ours for the taking. But what were we to *do*? Some few tasks appealed to us at once, since they lay ready to our hands. We descended into the kitchen and laid the two domestics upon their respective beds. They seemed to have died without suffering, one in the chair by the fire, the other upon the scullery floor. Then we carried in poor Austin from the yard. His muscles were set as hard as a board in the most exaggerated rigor mortis, while the contraction of the fibres had drawn his mouth into a hard sardonic grin. This symptom was prevalent among all who had died from the poison. Wherever we went we were confronted by those grinning faces, which seemed to mock at our dreadful position, smiling silently and grimly at the ill-fated survivors of their race.

'Look here,' said Lord John, who had paced restlessly about the dining room whilst we partook of some food, 'I don't know how you fellows feel about it, but for my part, I simply *can't* sit here and do nothin'.'

'Perhaps,' Challenger answered, 'you would have the kindness to suggest what you think we ought to do.'

'Get a move on us and see all that has happened.'

'That is what I should myself propose.'

'But not in this little country village. We can see from the window all that this place can teach us.'

'Where should we go, then?'

'To London!'

'That's all very well,' grumbled Summerlee. 'You may be equal to a forty mile walk, but I'm not so sure about Challenger, with his stumpy legs, and I am perfectly sure about myself.'

Challenger was very much annoyed.

'If you could see your way, sir, to confining your remarks to your own physical peculiarities, you would find that you had an ample field for comment,' he cried.

'I had no intention to offend you, my dear Challenger!' cried our tactless friend, 'You can't be held responsible for your own physique. If nature has given you a short, heavy body you cannot possibly help having stumpy legs.'

Challenger was too furious to answer. He could only growl and blink and bristle. Lord John hastened to intervene before the dispute became more violent.

'You talk of walking. Why should we walk?' said he.

'Do you suggest taking a train?' asked Challenger, still simmering.

'What's the matter with the motor car? Why should we not go in that?'

'I am not an expert,' said Challenger, pulling at his beard reflectively. 'At the same time, you are right in supposing that the human intellect in its higher manifestations should be sufficiently flexible to turn itself to anything. Your idea is an excellent one, Lord John. I myself will drive you all to London.'

'You will do nothing of the kind,' said Summerlee with decision.

'No, indeed, George!' cried his wife. 'You only tried once, and you remember how you crashed through the gate of the garage.'

'It was a momentary want of concentration,' said Challenger complacently. 'You can consider the matter settled. I will certainly drive you all to London.'

The situation was relieved by Lord John.

'What's the car?' he asked.

'A twenty-horse Humber.'

'Why, I've driven one for years,' said he. 'By George!' he added. 'I never thought I'd live to take the whole human race in one load. There's just room for five, as I remember it. Get your things on, and I'll be ready at the door by ten o'clock.'

Sure enough, at the hour named, the car came purring and crackling from the yard with Lord John at the wheel. I took my seat beside him, while the lady, a useful little buffer state, was squeezed in between the two men of wrath at the back. Then Lord John released his brakes, slid his lever rapidly from first to third, and we sped off upon the strangest drive that ever human beings have taken since man first came upon the earth.

You are to picture the loveliness of nature upon that August day, the freshness of the morning air, the golden glare of the summer sunshine, the cloudless sky, the luxuriant green of the Sussex woods, and the deep purple of heather-clad downs. As you looked round upon the many-coloured beauty of the scene all thought of a vast catastrophe would have passed from your mind had it not been for one sinister sign – the solemn, all-embracing silence. There is a gentle hum of life which pervades a closely settled country, so deep and constant that one ceases to observe it, as the dweller by the sea loses all sense of the constant murmur of the waves. The twitter of birds, the buzz of insects, the far-off echo of voices, the lowing of cattle, the distant barking of dogs, roar of trains, and rattle of carts – all these form one low, unremitting note, striking unheeded upon the ear. We missed it now. This deadly silence was appalling. So solemn was it, so impressive, that the buzz and rattle of our motor car seemed an unwarrantable intrusion, an indecent disregard of this reverent stillness which lay like a pall over and round the ruins of humanity. It was this grim hush, and the tall clouds of smoke which rose here and there over the countryside from smouldering buildings, which cast a chill into our hearts as we gazed round at the glorious panorama of the Weald.

And then there were the dead! At first those endless groups of drawn and grinning faces filled us with a shuddering horror. So vivid and mordant was the impression that I can live over again that slow descent of the station hill, the passing by the nurse girl with the two babes, the sight of the old horse on his knees between the shafts, the cabman twisted across his seat, and the young man inside with his hand upon the open door in the very act of springing out. Lower down were six reapers all in a litter, their limbs crossing, their dead, unwinking eyes gazing upwards at the glare of heaven. These things I see as in a photograph. But soon, by the merciful provision of nature, the overexcited nerve ceased to respond. The very vastness of the horror took away from its personal appeal. Individuals merged into groups, groups into crowds, crowds into a universal phenomenon which one soon accepted as the inevitable detail of every scene. Only here and there, where some particularly brutal or grotesque incident caught the attention, did the mind come back with a sudden shock to the personal and human meaning of it all.

Above all, there was the fate of the children. That, I remember, filled us with the strongest sense of intolerable injustice. We could have wept – Mrs Challenger did weep – when we passed a great council school and saw the long trail of tiny figures scattered down the road which led from it. They had been dismissed by their terrified teachers and were speeding for their homes when the poison caught them in its net. Great numbers of people were at the open windows of the houses. In Tunbridge Wells there was hardly one which had not its staring, smiling face. At the last instant the need of air, that very craving for oxygen which we alone had been able to satisfy, had sent them flying to the window. The sidewalks too were littered with men and women, hatless and bonnetless, who had rushed out of the houses. Many of them had fallen in the roadway. It was a lucky thing that in Lord John we had found an expert driver, for it was no easy matter to pick one's way. Passing through the villages or towns we could only go at a walking pace, and once, I remember, opposite the school at Tonbridge, we had to halt some time while we carried aside the bodies which blocked our path.

A few small, definite pictures stand out in my memory from amid that long panorama of death upon the Sussex and Kentish high roads. One was that of a great, glittering motor car standing outside the inn at the village of Southborough. It bore, as I should guess, some pleasure party upon their return from Brighton or from Eastbourne. There were three gaily dressed women, all young and beautiful, one of them with a Peking spaniel upon her lap. With them were a rakish-looking elderly man and a young aristocrat, his eyeglass still in his eye, his cigarette burned down to the stub between the fingers of his begloved hand. Death must have come on them in an instant and fixed them as they sat. Save that the elderly man had at the last moment torn out his collar in an effort to breathe, they might all have been asleep. On one side of the car a waiter with some broken glasses beside a tray was huddled near the step. On the other, two very ragged tramps, a man and a woman, lay where they had fallen, the man with his long, thin arm still outstretched, even as he had asked for alms in his lifetime. One instant of time had put aristocrat, waiter, tramp, and dog upon one common footing of inert and dissolving protoplasm.

I remember another singular picture, some miles on the London side of Sevenoaks. There is a large convent upon the left, with a long, green slope in front of it. Upon this slope were assembled a great number of school children, all kneeling at prayer. In front of them was a fringe of nuns, and higher up the slope, facing towards them, a single figure whom we took to be the Mother Superior. Unlike the pleasure-seekers in the motor car, these people seemed to have had warning of their danger and to have died beautifully together, the teachers and the taught, assembled for their last common lesson.

My mind is still stunned by that terrific experience, and I grope vainly for means of expression by which I can reproduce the emotions which we felt. Perhaps it is best and wisest not to try, but merely to indicate the facts. Even Summerlee and Challenger were crushed, and we heard nothing of our companions behind us save an occasional whimper from the lady. As to Lord John, he was too intent upon his wheel and the difficult task of threading his way along such roads to have time or inclination for conversation. One phrase he used with such wearisome iteration that it stuck in my memory and at last almost made me laugh as a comment upon the day of doom.

'Pretty doin's! What!'

That was his ejaculation as each fresh tremendous combination of death and disaster displayed itself before us. 'Pretty doin's! What!' he cried, as we descended the station hill at Rotherfield, and it was still 'Pretty doin's! What!' as we picked our way through a wilderness of death in the High Street of Lewisham and the Old Kent Road.

It was here that we received a sudden and amazing shock. Out of the window of a humble corner house there appeared a fluttering handkerchief waving at the end of a long, thin human arm. Never had the sight of unexpected death caused our hearts to stop and then throb so wildly as did this amazing indication of life. Lord John ran the motor to the kerb, and in an instant we had rushed through the open door of the house and up the staircase to the second-floor front room from which the signal proceeded.

A very old lady sat in a chair by the open window, and close to her, laid across a second chair, was a cylinder of oxygen, smaller but of the same shape as those which had saved our own lives. She turned her thin, drawn, bespectacled face toward us as we crowded in at the doorway.

'I feared that I was abandoned here forever,' said she, 'for I am an invalid and cannot stir.'

'Well, madam,' Challenger answered, 'it is a lucky chance that we happened to pass.'

'I have one all-important question to ask you,' said she. 'Gentlemen, I beg that you will be frank with me. What effect will these events have upon London and North-Western Railway shares?'

We should have laughed had it not been for the tragic eagerness with which she listened for our answer. Mrs Burston, for that was her name, was an aged widow, whose whole income depended upon a small holding of this stock. Her life had been regulated by the rise and fall of the dividend, and she could form no conception of existence save as it was affected by the quotation of her shares. In vain we pointed out to her that all the money in the world was hers for the taking and was useless when taken. Her old mind would not adapt itself to the new idea, and she wept loudly over her vanished stock. 'It was all I had,' she wailed. 'If that is gone I may as well go too.'

Amid her lamentations we found out how this frail old plant had lived where the whole great forest had fallen. She was a confirmed invalid and an asthmatic. Oxygen had been prescribed for her malady, and a tube was in her room at the moment of the crisis. She had naturally inhaled some as had been her habit when there was a difficulty with her breathing. It had given her relief, and by doling out her supply she had managed to survive the night. Finally she had fallen asleep and been awakened by the buzz of our motor car. As it was impossible to take her on with us, we saw that she had all necessaries of life and promised to communicate with her in a couple of days at the latest. So we left her, still weeping bitterly over her vanished stock.

As we approached the Thames the block in the streets became thicker and the obstacles more bewildering. It was with difficulty that we made our way across London Bridge. The approaches to it upon the Middlesex side were choked from end to end with frozen traffic which made all further advance in that direction impossible. A ship was blazing brightly alongside one of the wharves near the bridge, and the air was full of drifting smuts and of a heavy acrid smell of burning. There was a cloud of dense smoke somewhere near the Houses of Parliament, but it was impossible from where we were to see what was on fire.

'I don't know how it strikes you,' Lord John remarked as he brought his engine to a standstill, 'but it seems to me the country is more cheerful than the town. Dead London is gettin' on my nerves. I'm for a cast round and then gettin' back to Rotherfield.'

'I confess that I do not see what we can hope for here,' said Professor Summerlee.

'At the same time,' said Challenger, his great voice booming strangely amid the silence, 'it is difficult for us to conceive that out of seven millions of people there is only this one old woman who by some peculiarity of constitution or some accident of occupation has managed to survive this catastrophe.'

'If there should be others, how can we hope to find them, George?' asked the lady. 'And yet I agree with you that we cannot go back until we have tried.'

Getting out of the car and leaving it by the kerb, we walked with some difficulty along the crowded pavement of King William Street and entered the open door of a large insurance office. It was a corner house, and we chose it as commanding a view in every direction. Ascending the stair, we passed through what I suppose to have been the boardroom, for eight elderly men were seated round a long table in the centre of it. The high window was open and we all stepped out upon the balcony. From it we could see the crowded city streets radiating in every direction, while below us the road was black from side to side with the tops of the motionless taxis. All, or nearly all, had their heads pointed outwards, showing how the terrified men of the city had at the last moment made a vain endeavour to rejoin their families in the suburbs or the country. Here and there amid the humbler cabs towered the great brass-spangled motor car of some wealthy magnate, wedged hopelessly among the dammed stream of arrested traffic. Just beneath us there was such a one of great size and luxurious appearance, with its owner, a fat old man, leaning out, half his gross body through the window, and his podgy hand, gleaming with diamonds, outstretched as he urged his chauffeur to make a last effort to break through the press.

A dozen motor buses towered up like islands in this flood, the passengers who crowded the roofs lying all huddled together and across each other's laps like a child's toys in a nursery. On a broad lamp pedestal in the centre of the roadway, a burly policeman was standing, leaning his back against the post in so natural an attitude that it was hard to realise that he was not alive, while at his feet there lay a ragged newsboy with his bundle of papers on the ground beside him. A paper-cart had got blocked in the crowd, and we could read in large letters, black upon yellow, 'Scene at Lord's. County Match Interrupted.' This must have been the earliest edition, for there were other placards bearing the legend, 'Is It the End? Great Scientist's Warning.' And another, 'Is Challenger Justified? Ominous Rumours.'

Challenger pointed the latter placard out to his wife, as it thrust itself like a banner above the throng. I could see him throw out his chest and stroke his beard as he looked at it. It pleased and flattered that complex mind to think that London had died with his name and his words still present in their thoughts. His feelings were so evident that they aroused the sardonic comment of his colleague.

'In the limelight to the last, Challenger,' he remarked.

'So it would appear,' he answered complacently. 'Well,' he added as he looked down the long vista of the radiating streets, all silent and all choked up with death, 'I really see no purpose to be served by our staying any longer in London. I suggest that we return at once to Rotherfield and then take counsel as to how we shall most profitably employ the years which lie before us.'

Only one other picture shall I give of the scenes which we carried back in our memories from the dead city. It is a glimpse which we had of the interior of the old church of St Mary's, which is at the very point where our car was awaiting us. Picking our way among the prostrate figures upon the steps, we pushed open the swing door and entered. It was a wonderful sight. The church was crammed from end to end with kneeling figures in every posture of supplication and abasement. At the last dreadful moment, brought suddenly face to face with the realities of life, those terrific realities which hang over us even while we follow the shadows, the terrified people had rushed into those old city churches which for generations had hardly ever held a congregation. There they huddled as close as they could kneel, many of them in their agitation still wearing their hats, while above them in the pulpit a young man in lay dress had apparently been addressing them when he and they had been overwhelmed by the same fate. He lay now, like Punch in his booth, with his head and two limp arms hanging over the ledge of the pulpit. It was a nightmare, the grey, dusty church, the rows of agonised figures, the dimness and silence of it all. We moved about with hushed whispers, walking upon our tiptoes.

And then suddenly I had an idea. At one corner of the church, near the door, stood the ancient font, and behind it a deep recess in which there hung the ropes for the bell-ringers. Why should we not send a message out over London which would attract to us anyone who might still be alive? I ran across, and pulling at the list-covered rope, I was surprised to find how difficult it was to swing the bell. Lord John had followed me.

'By George, young fellah!' said he, pulling off his coat. 'You've hit on a dooced good notion. Give me a grip and we'll soon have a move on it.'

But, even then, so heavy was the bell that it was not until Challenger and Summerlee had added their weight to ours that we heard the roaring and clanging above our heads which told us that the great clapper was ringing out its music. Far over dead London resounded our message of comradeship and hope to any fellow man surviving. It cheered our own hearts, that strong, metallic call, and we turned the more earnestly to our work, dragged two feet off the earth with each upward jerk of the rope, but all straining together on the downward heave, Challenger the lowest of all, bending all his great strength to the task and flopping up and down like a monstrous bullfrog, croaking with every pull. It was at that moment that an artist might have taken a picture of the four adventurers, the comrades of many strange perils in the past, whom Fate had now chosen for so supreme an experience. For half an hour we worked, the sweat dropping from our faces, our arms and backs aching with the exertion. Then we went out into the portico of the church and looked eagerly up and down the silent, crowded streets. Not a sound, not a motion, in answer to our summons.

'It's no use. No one is left,' I cried.

'We can do nothing more,' said Mrs Challenger. 'For God's sake, George, let us get back to Rotherfield. Another hour of this dreadful, silent city would drive me mad.'

We got into the car without another word. Lord John backed her round and turned her to the south. To us the chapter seemed closed. Little did we foresee the strange new chapter which was to open.

6

The Great Awakening

And now I come to the end of this extraordinary incident, so overshadowing in its importance, not only in our own small, individual lives, but in the general history of the human race. As I said when I began my narrative, when that history comes to be written, this occurrence will surely stand out among all other events like a mountain towering among its foothills. Our generation has been reserved for a very special fate since it has been chosen to experience so wonderful a thing. How long its effect may last – how long mankind may preserve the humility and reverence which this great shock has taught it – can only be shown by the future. I think it is safe to say that things can never be quite the same again. Never can one realise how powerless and ignorant one is, and how one is upheld by an unseen hand, until for an instant that hand has seemed to close and to crush. Death has been imminent upon us. We know that at any moment it may be again. That grim presence shadows our lives, but who can deny that in that shadow the sense of duty, the feeling of sobriety and responsibility, the appreciation of the gravity and of the objects of life, the earnest desire to develop and improve, have grown and become real with us to a degree that has leavened our whole society from end to end? It is something beyond sects and beyond dogmas. It is rather an alteration of perspective, a shifting of our sense of proportion, a vivid realisation that we are insignificant and evanescent creatures, existing on sufferance and at the mercy of the first chill wind from the unknown. But if the world has grown graver with this knowledge it is not, I think, a sadder place in consequence. Surely we are agreed that the more sober and restrained pleasures of the present are deeper as well as wiser than the noisy, foolish hustle which passed so often for enjoyment in the days of old – days so recent and yet already so inconceivable. Those empty lives which were wasted in aimless visiting and being visited, in the worry of great and unnecessary households, in the arranging and eating of elaborate and tedious meals, have now found rest and health in the reading, the music, the gentle family communion which comes from a simpler and saner division of their time. With greater health and greater pleasure they are richer than before, even after they have paid those increased contributions to the common fund which have so raised the standard of life in these islands.

There is some clash of opinion as to the exact hour of the great awakening. It is generally agreed that, apart from the difference of clocks, there may have been local causes which influenced the action of the poison. Certainly, in each separate district the resurrection was practically simultaneous. There are numerous witnesses that Big Ben pointed to ten minutes past six at the moment. The Astronomer Royal has fixed the Greenwich time at twelve past six. On the other hand, Laird Johnson, a very capable East Anglia observer, has recorded six-twenty as the hour. In the Hebrides it was as late as seven. In our own case there can be no doubt whatever, for I was seated in Challenger's study with his carefully tested chronometer in front of me at the moment. The hour was a quarter past six.

An enormous depression was weighing upon my spirits. The cumulative effect of all the dreadful sights which we had seen upon our journey was heavy upon my soul. With my abounding animal health and great physical energy any kind of mental clouding was a rare event. I had the Irish faculty of seeing some gleam of humour in every darkness. But now the obscurity was appalling and unrelieved. The others were downstairs making their plans for the future. I sat by the open window, my chin resting upon my hand and my mind absorbed in the misery of our situation. Could we continue to live? That was the question which I had begun to ask myself. Was it possible to exist upon a dead world? Just as in physics the greater body draws to itself the lesser, would we not feel an overpowering attraction from that vast body of humanity which had passed into the unknown? How would the end come? Would it be from a return of the poison? Or would the earth be uninhabitable from the mephitic products of universal decay? Or, finally, might our awful situation prey upon and unbalance our minds? A group of insane folk upon a dead world! My mind was brooding upon this last dreadful idea when some slight noise caused me to look down upon the road beneath me. The old cab horse was coming up the hill!

I was conscious at the same instant of the twittering of birds, of someone coughing in the yard below, and of a background of movement in the landscape. And yet I remember that it was that absurd, emaciated, superannuated cab horse which held my gaze. Slowly and wheezily it was climbing the slope. Then my eye travelled to the driver sitting hunched up upon the box and finally to the young man who was leaning out of the window in some excitement and shouting a direction. They were all indubitably, aggressively alive!

Everybody was alive once more! Had it all been a delusion? Was it conceivable that this whole poison belt incident had been an elaborate dream? For an instant my startled brain was really ready to believe it. Then I looked down, and there was the rising blister on my hand where it was frayed by the rope of the city bell. It had really been so, then. And yet here was the world resuscitated – here was life come back in an instant full tide to the planet. Now, as my eyes wandered all over the great landscape, I saw it in every direction – and moving, to my amazement, in the very same groove in which it had halted. There were the golfers. Was it possible that they were going on with their game? Yes, there was a fellow driving off from a tee, and that other group upon the green were surely putting for the hole. The reapers were slowly trooping back to their work. The nurse girl slapped one of her charges and then began to push the perambulator up the hill. Everyone had unconcernedly taken up the thread at the very point where they had dropped it.

I rushed downstairs, but the hall door was open, and I heard the voices of my companions, loud in astonishment and con-gratulation, in the yard. How we all shook hands and laughed as we came together, and how Mrs Challenger kissed us all in her emotion, before she finally threw herself into the bear-hug of her husband.

'But they could not have been asleep!' cried Lord John. 'Dash it all, Challenger, you don't mean to believe that those folk were asleep with their staring eyes and stiff limbs and that awful death grin on their faces!'

'It can only have been the condition that is called catalepsy,' said Challenger. 'It has been a rare phenomenon in the past and has constantly been mistaken for death. While it endures, the temperature falls, the respiration disappears, the heartbeat is indistinguishable – in fact, it *is* death, save that it is evanescent. Even the most comprehensive mind' – here he closed his eyes and simpered – 'could hardly conceive a universal outbreak of it in this fashion.'

'You may label it catalepsy,' remarked Summerlee, 'but, after all, that is only a name, and we know as little of the result as we do of the poison which has caused it. The most we can say is that the vitiated ether has produced a temporary death.'

Austin was seated all in a heap on the step of the car. It was his coughing which I had heard from above. He had been hold-ing his head in silence, but now he was muttering to himself and running his eyes over the car.

'Young fat-head!' he grumbled. 'Can't leave things alone!'

'What's the matter, Austin?'

'Lubricators left running, sir. Someone has been fooling with the car. I expect it's that young garden boy, sir.'

Lord John looked guilty.

'I don't know what's amiss with me,' continued Austin, staggering to his feet. 'I expect I came over queer when I was hosing her down. I seem to remember flopping over by the step. But I'll swear I never left those lubricator taps on.'

In a condensed narrative the astonished Austin was told what had happened to himself and the world. The mystery of the dripping lubricators was also explained to him. He listened with an air of deep distrust when told how an amateur had driven his car and with absorbed interest to the few sentences in which our experiences of the sleeping city were recorded. I can remember his comment when the story was concluded.

'Was you outside the Bank of England, sir?'

'Yes, Austin.'

'With all them millions inside and everybody asleep?'

'That was so.'

'And I not there!' he groaned, and turned dismally once more to the hosing of his car.

There was a sudden grinding of wheels upon gravel. The old cab had actually pulled up at Challenger's door. I saw the young occupant step out from it. An instant later the maid, who looked as tousled and bewildered as if she had that instant been roused from the deepest sleep, appeared with a card upon a tray. Challenger snorted ferociously as he looked at it, and his thick black hair seemed to bristle up in his wrath.

'A pressman!' he growled. Then, with a deprecating smile: 'After all, it is natural that the whole world should hasten to know what I think of such an episode.'

'That can hardly be his errand,' said Summerlee, 'for he was on the road in his cab before ever the crisis came.'

I looked at the card: 'James Baxter, London Correspondent, *New York Monitor*.'

'You'll see him?' said I.

'Not I.'

'Oh, George! You should be kinder and more considerate to others. Surely you have learned something from what we have undergone.'

He tut-tutted and shook his big, obstinate head.

'A poisonous breed! Eh, Malone? The worst weed in modern civilisation, the ready tool of the quack and the hindrance of the self-respecting man! When did they ever say a good word for me?'

'When did you ever say a good word to them?' I answered. 'Come, sir, this is a stranger who has made a journey to see you. I am sure that you won't be rude to him.'

'Well, well,' he grumbled, 'you come with me and do the talking. I protest in advance against any such outrageous invasion of my private life.' Muttering and mumbling, he came rolling after me like an angry and rather ill-conditioned mastiff.

The dapper young American pulled out his notebook and plunged instantly into his subject.

'I came down, sir,' said he, 'because our people in America would very much like to hear more about this danger which is, in your opinion, pressing upon the world.'

'I know of no danger which is now pressing upon the world,' Challenger answered gruffly.

The pressman looked at him in mild surprise.

'I meant, sir, the chances that the world might run into a belt of poisonous ether.'

'I do not now apprehend any such danger,' said Challenger.

The pressman looked even more perplexed.

'You are Professor Challenger, are you not?' he asked.

'Yes, sir; that is my name.'

'I cannot understand, then, how you can say that there is no such danger. I am alluding to your own letter, published above your name in the London *Times* of this morning.'

It was Challenger's turn to look surprised.

'This morning?' said he. 'No London *Times* was published this morning.'

'Surely, sir,' said the American in mild remonstrance, 'you must admit that the London *Times* is a daily paper.' He drew out a copy from his inside pocket. 'Here is the letter to which I refer.'

Challenger chuckled and rubbed his hands.

'I begin to understand,' said he. 'So you read this letter this morning?'

'Yes, sir.'

'And came at once to interview me?'

'Yes, sir.'

'Did you observe anything unusual upon the journey down?'

'Well, to tell the truth, your people seemed more lively and generally human than I have ever seen them. The baggage man set out to tell me a funny story, and that's a new experience for me in this country.'

'Nothing else?'

'Why, no, sir, not that I can recall.'

'Well, now, what hour did you leave Victoria?'

The American smiled.

'I came here to interview you, Professor, but you're doing most of the work.'

'It happens to interest me. Do you recall the hour?'

'Sure. It was half past twelve.'

'And you arrived?'

'At a quarter past two.'

'And you hired a cab?'

'That was so.'

'How far do you suppose it is to the station?'

'Well, I should reckon the best part of two miles.'

'So how long do you think it took you?'

'Well, half an hour, maybe, with that asthmatic in front.'

'So it should be three o'clock?'

'Yes, or a trifle after it.'

'Look at your watch.'

The American did so and then stared at us in astonishment.

'Say!' he cried. 'It's run down. That horse has broken every record, sure. The sun is pretty low, now that I come to look at it. Well, there's something here I don't understand.'

'Have you no remembrance of anything remarkable as you came up the hill?'

'Well, I seem to recollect that I was mighty sleepy once. It comes back to me that I wanted to say something to the driver and that I couldn't make him heed me. I guess it was the heat, but I felt swimmy for a moment. That's all.'

'So it is with the whole human race,' said Challenger to me. 'They have all felt swimmy for a moment. None of them have as yet any comprehension of what has occurred. Each will go on with his interrupted job as Austin has snatched up his hose-pipe or the golfer continued his game. Your editor, Malone, will continue the issue of his papers, and very much amazed he will be at finding that an issue is missing. Yes, my young friend,' he added to the American reporter, with a sudden mood of amused geniality, 'it may interest you to know that the world has swum through the poisonous current which swirls like the Gulf Stream through the ocean of ether. You will also kindly note for your own future convenience that today is not Friday, August the twenty-seventh, but Saturday, August the twenty-eighth, and that you sat senseless in your cab for twenty-eight hours upon the Rotherfield hill.'

And 'right here', as my American colleague would say, I may bring this narrative to an end. It is, as you are probably aware, only a fuller and more detailed version of the account which appeared in the Monday edition of the *Daily Gazette* – an account which has been universally admitted to be the greatest journalistic scoop of all time, which sold no fewer than three and a half million copies of the paper. Framed upon the wall of my sanctum I retain those magnificent headlines: –

TWENTY-EIGHT HOURS' WORLD COMA
UNPRECEDENTED EXPERIENCE
CHALLENGER JUSTIFIED
OUR CORRESPONDENT ESCAPES
ENTHRALLING NARRATIVE
THE OXYGEN ROOM
WEIRD MOTOR DRIVE
DEAD LONDON
REPLACING THE MISSING PAGE
GREAT FIRES AND LOSS OF LIFE
WILL IT RECUR?

Underneath this glorious scroll came nine and a half columns of narrative, in which appeared the first, last, and only account of the history of the planet, so far as one observer could draw it, during one long day of its existence. Challenger and Summerlee have treated the matter in a joint scientific paper, but to me alone was left the popular account. Surely I can sing '*Nunc dimittis*'. What is left but anti-climax in the life of a journalist after that!

But let me not end on sensational headlines and a merely personal triumph. Rather let me quote the sonorous passages in which the greatest of daily papers ended its admirable leader upon the subject – a leader which might well be filed for reference by every thoughtful man.

'It has been a well-worn truism,' said The Times, 'that our human race are a feeble folk before the infinite latent forces which surround us. From the prophets of old and from the philosophers of our own time the same message and warning have reached us. But, like all oft-repeated truths, it has in time lost something of its actuality and cogency. A lesson, an actual experience, was needed to bring it home. It is from that salutory but terrible ordeal that we have just emerged, with minds which are still stunned by the suddenness of the blow and with spirits which are chastened by the realisation of our own limitations and impotence. The world has paid a fearful price for its schooling. Hardly yet have we learned the full tale of disaster, but the destruction by fire of New York, of Orleans, and of Brighton constitutes in itself one of the greatest tragedies in the history of our race. When the account of the railway and shipping accidents has been completed, it will furnish grim reading, although there is evidence to show that in the vast majority of cases the drivers of trains and engineers of steamers succeeded in shutting off their motive power before succumbing to the poison. But the material damage, enormous as it is both in life and in property, is not the consideration which will be uppermost in our minds today. All this may in time be forgotten. But what will not be forgotten, and what will and should continue to obsess our imaginations, is this revelation of the possibilities of the universe, this destruction of our ignorant self-complacency, and this demonstration of how narrow is the path of our material existence and what abysses may lie upon either side of it. Solemnity and humility are at the base of all our emotions today. May they be the foundations upon which a more earnest and reverent race may build a more worthy temple.'

Biographical Note

Arthur Conan Doyle was born in Edinburgh in 1859. His father was Charles Altamont Doyle, son of the caricaturist John Doyle, and his mother an Irish woman, Mary Foley. The young Conan Doyle was brought up in the Catholic faith and, at the age of nine, was sent to Stonyhurst College, a Jesuit school in Lancashire. Here he began to write verse and was editor of the school newspaper, but his time at the school was largely unhappy and, by the time he left in 1875, the severe regime had caused him to reject his beliefs and become agnostic.

Conan Doyle went on to study medicine at Edinburgh University, though he continued to write, and was employed as surgeon's clerk by the impressive and ingenious Dr Joseph Bell, who was to become the model for Conan Doyle's own Sherlock Holmes. He took several jobs during his time at Edinburgh and served as surgeon on a number of seagoing expeditions, including, in 1881, a voyage to the west coast of Africa, where he stayed with the black abolitionist leader Henry Highland Garnet.

In 1882, Conan Doyle moved to Southsea to set up his own medical practice and it was here, in his quieter moments, that he began to focus on his writing. He married Louise Hawkins, the sister of one of his patients, in 1886, and in 1887 the first Sherlock Holmes novel, *A Study in Scarlet*, was published in *Beeton's Christmas Annual*.

Louise's health was unstable, and in 1895 the Doyles left England for Egypt in the hope of finding a cure for her tuberculosis, and here, amidst the fighting between the dervishes and the English, the idea for *The Tragedy of the Korosko* was conceived. Conan Doyle was an avid supporter of the British Army in Africa, and though his attempts to enlist were unsuccessful, his tract *The War in South Africa: Its Cause and Conduct*

(1902) was extremely influential and translated into several languages. He twice stood for Parliament in the early 1900s, and became a prominent campaigner for victims of injustice.

The widowed Conan Doyle remarried in 1907 and moved to Crowborough in Sussex and during the latter part of his life devoted himself to the promulgation of the spiritualism he had first discovered at Southsea; he wrote prodigiously, including the Professor Challenger series and *The History of Spiritualism* (1926), and embarked on a series of lecture tours. His beliefs conflicted with those of many of his peers, but it was the controversy of the Cottingley fairy photographs, which Conan Doyle declared to be genuine, that has proved to be the lasting legacy of these final years. Conan Doyle died of a heart attack at Crowborough in 1930.